JUDITH CASELEY

Harry and Arney

Greenwillow Books, New York

Library of Congress Cataloging-in-Publication Data
Caseley, Judith.
  Harry and Arney / by Judith Caseley.
     p.   cm.
  Summary: Six-year-old Harry looks forward to having a new baby brother, but after his arrival, Harry discovers that he is glad to have his two older sisters around.
  ISBN 0-688-12140-3
  [1. Babies—Fiction.
2. Brothers and sisters—Fiction.
3. Family life—Fiction.]
I. Title.
PZ7.C2677Hap   1994
[Fic]—dc20
93-20787   CIP   AC

For SCH,
with love again

Contents

1

Harry's Bonemeal

HARRY KNEW in his heart that his mother was having a baby boy instead of a baby girl. She just had to. After all, the family would be lopsided if Mrs. Kane had a girl. Harry already had two older sisters, Chloe and Dorothy, and two was enough. One more annoying sister combing her hair in the bathroom or putting her Feed Me Baby right next to him at the kitchen table with pink stuff dribbling down her mouth would be more than he could stand.

Ever since the Kane family had moved from an apartment to a house, which meant that he no longer shared a room with his sister Dorothy, he had been lonely. And when his pet turtle, Personality, had escaped from his tank and ended up a shriveled shell in the dryer, Harry was even lonelier. A new baby meant that Harry was no longer going to be alone. But it also meant that he would no longer be the baby in the family. So in the beginning, Harry had boycotted the baby. He didn't talk about it or think about it. That is, until he figured out with his own special scientific theory that the baby was going to be a boy. A boy baby might be fun. And Harry had some boy tricks up his sleeve that only a baby brother would understand.

Early in December, when the telephone rang, Harry picked it up on the second ring and said, "Hello, who is it?" without waiting for the person on the other end of the line to speak. He leaned across his sister Chloe, flapping the telephone wire annoyingly across her cheek while she tried to work on her homework at the kitchen table.

"You're choking me with that cord," complained Chloe, pulling the curlicued wire away from her.

"Who is it, Harry?" his mother called from the living room.

"It's Dr. Shapiro," said Harry, jiggling the telephone cord so that it danced on top of Chloe's head.

"He's bothering me with the phone," shouted Chloe.

"He's bothering her with the phone," repeated Dorothy, who was sitting across from her sister drinking a glass of chocolate milk.

"What are you, an echo?" said Harry, holding out the receiver to his mother and thinking that if he had a brother, a brother would surely understand that tapping a springy wire on top of someone's head was a form of making music, not grounds for tattling.

"Wait for the person to answer before you ask who it is," said Mrs. Kane, pushing herself off the couch. "And stop torturing your sister."

"My mother's having a baby." Harry spoke into the telephone before his mother could reach him.

"He knows that," said Chloe. "He's her baby doctor."

"Shush," said Mrs. Kane as she took the receiver. "Hello, Dr. Shapiro." She listened, looking very serious for a moment, and then she smiled. "I see. Wonderful. Terrific."

"What?" said Harry, tugging on his mother's sleeve. "The baby is coming?"

Mrs. Kane cupped her hand over the receiver. "The test says that the baby is definitely a boy," she whispered. "Thank you, Doctor," she spoke into the telephone, but before she could hang up, Harry grabbed it.

"Dr. Shapiro?" said Harry. "It's Harry, the baby's big brother who happens to be a scientist. I knew it was a boy already."

Harry listened intently. Then he beamed and said, "Because her tummy looks just like a basketball. And I love watching basketball, and playing basketball, and so does my father, and he's a boy and I'm a boy, so it has to be a boy. Good-bye." Harry hung up the telephone.

"It's polite to say good-bye and wait for an answer," said Mrs. Kane. "And it's not polite to grab the phone from someone."

"Sorry," said Harry. "But I thought he'd like to

know my scientific theory, so other families could find out if it was a boy or a girl."

Mrs. Kane laughed. "What did the doctor say about your theory?" she said.

Harry waved a hand through the air and said, "Doctors don't know everything."

"What did he say?" said Chloe, putting down her pencil.

"He said that girls like basketball, too."

"He's right," said Mrs. Kane.

"I'm more right," said Harry, grabbing an apple from a basket on the table, "because in our family, girls don't much like basketball."

"I knew Mom was having a boy before anybody," said Chloe. "Because we found out when I went with her to get her test at the hospital."

"My amniocentesis," said Mrs. Kane. "When you finish that apple, put the apple core in the garbage can."

Harry took a big bite and patted his mother's stomach. "Hello, Mr. Basketball," he said. "Harry the Scientist knew you were a boy baby before anybody." He raced into the living room and twirled in his socks like a hockey player on ice.

"I'm going to keep the apple core for an experiment!" Harry shouted from the other room.

His mother sighed. Chloe and Dorothy joined her. "What kind of experiment?" called Mrs. Kane wearily.

Harry popped his head around the corner. "A compost heap," he said. "I could put the old food into Personality's old turtle tank and let it rot, and then we could use it to make the soil richer in the garden and for our plants, too."

Chloe sounded like her mother. "Just what we need," she said. "An experiment in stinkiness."

"An experiment in grossness," added Dorothy, rolling her eyes.

"Then I'll do it in the back of the garden," said Harry, grabbing his jacket and running into the bedroom. "I have my tank, I have my apple core. I'm in business," he announced gleefully as he staggered out of the room carrying a heavy glass tank.

Mrs. Kane sat back in her chair and reached for

an apple. She bit into it. "There," she said. "A few more bites and I'll have some more scientific material for Professor Harry Albert Einstein's experiment."

Dorothy put her chin in her hand. "Professor Harry Albert Einstein's experiment in grossness," she repeated.

Harry worked diligently on his compost heap for several days. When his mother wasn't looking, he sneaked cooked string beans into his napkin at suppertime and deposited them in Personality's tank at the back of the garden. He layered the mixture with an occasional gob of oatmeal when he could manage it, a scattering of raisins, some carrot scrapings, potato peels, orange rind, and the daily remains of his lunch box.

His oldest sister, Chloe, couldn't have cared less about Harry's compost heap, but Dorothy was interested enough to note that Harry's heap was exactly the same kind of mixture that the farmer in the film she had seen at school had fed his pigs.

Harry was thoughtful for a moment and said, "Why do you think they call them pigs? Who else would eat that stuff?"

A few weeks later, when his mother was in the basement doing laundry, Harry took his napkin of lunchtime leftovers and dug them into his mother's potted tree in the living room.

"You don't look well at all," whispered Harry.

Dorothy stood guard. "Make sure the orange peel isn't showing," she cautioned. "Mama wouldn't like it."

Harry regarded the drooping tree. "You'll be better in no time," he said, stroking a wilted leaf. "Harry's healthy compost heap will fix you right up."

Dorothy wasn't convinced. "I think she looks a little worse," she said, pointing out a few more wilted leaves.

The next time Mrs. Kane watered it, Harry stood by her side, making sure that the water didn't uncover any rotting orange peel. His mother mumbled, "This plant is not doing well at all." She didn't seem to notice the odd smell coming from the pot, and Harry decided not to mention it.

After a while, with eight days of Hanukkah, and winter vacation and two days of snow and starting back at school again, Harry forgot about the tree and he forgot about his compost heap. Then there was Valentine's Day and reading enough books so that he could earn a free pizza from the Pizza Shack, and Benjamin's birthday bowling party and President's Day. By March, the potted tree was a potted mess, with drooping branches and shriveled leaves.

"I don't know how I did it," Mrs. Kane said to Harry as he helped her drag it outside to the garbage can, "but somehow I managed to kill this poor little thing off."

Harry patted the top of the wilted tree and whispered, "Good-bye, old friend. We tried to make you better."

Mrs. Kane patted the top of Harry's head in much the same way. "Don't worry, sweetheart," she said. "I've bought us a new potted tree and some flowering plants in time for the baby's arrival."

"Do babies like plants and flowers?" said Harry.

"Babies are interested in the world," said Mrs.

Kane, grabbing his hand and swinging it. "Just you wait, Harry."

Waiting was not the easiest thing in the world for Harry. But it was almost springtime, which meant that it was almost time for Harry's new baby brother to be born, and Harry was determined to welcome him into this world with the healthiest plants and flowers that an older brother could arrange.

"My science teacher, Mr. Gezzik, says that a lot of gardeners use bonemeal," Harry told Dorothy as they walked home from school. "Maybe that's how come my compost heap didn't help the tree in the living room."

"That again?" said Dorothy. "Mom's plants look pretty healthy right now," she added doubtfully.

"You killed the last one," said Chloe, putting in her oldest sister's two cents. "Leave the new ones alone."

Harry kept right on talking about it through cartoons. "You dig a hole and you put this bonemeal stuff right into the soil. Do you think the reason they call it bonemeal is because the plants need a good, healthy meal? I think so. They were tired of all those apple cores and orange peels I gave them. They needed a change."

"We're having chicken tonight," said Dorothy, sniffing the air. "I'll save you my chicken bones."

"That's what they need!" said Harry, jumping into the air. "A good chicken-bone dinner. I'll get Chloe's bones, too. Mom's plants and flowers will be healthier than ever before. The pink will be pinker and the yellow will be yellower and the green will be greener and the baby will be born into the most beautiful world you ever saw."

"Then just don't take him into your room," said Dorothy. "It's a mess. And I wouldn't tell Mama."

"Don't tell Mama what?" said Mrs. Kane as she walked into the living room carrying a stack of folded laundry.

Harry sat down again. He looked at his mother's round stomach. "That my room is so messy it will scare the baby," he said.

Mrs. Kane smiled. "It will get messier," she said. "By springtime, the baby will be sharing your room." Harry's mother held out a pile of shirts to him. "Now put these away before then," she said, consulting her watch. "Your father has a meeting tonight, so we'll have an early dinner."

Harry had three whole pieces of his mother's famous honey-glazed chicken for supper. "That's the most chicken I've ever eaten in six years," said Harry, putting a drumstick bone on top of a pile of bones.

"You've only been on this planet for six years," said Chloe, wiping her hands with her napkin.

"Babies don't eat chicken for a long time, do they?" said Dorothy.

Mrs. Kane laughed. "Harry always loved chicken," she said. "Every week, Grandma Rebecca gave me a container of homemade chicken soup, with whole pieces of chicken in it, and I used to put it in the blender and feed it to Harry." She reached over and chucked Harry under the chin. "You used to spit out the chicken from the store-bought jars."

"I saw that kind in the jar at Mei-Hua's house when they were feeding Mei-Lun," said Chloe. "It looked disgusting. It smelled like dog food."

"Well, I hope this baby will eat it," said Mrs. Kane, rubbing her stomach. "The blender broke years ago, and I've no intention of getting another one." She stood up and started scraping the remains from Chloe's plate onto her own.

"I have an idea," said Harry, pushing himself away from the table. "You go rest, and we'll clean up all by ourselves."

"We will?" said Chloe.

"We will?" said Dorothy.

Harry cupped his hands around Dorothy's ear and whispered, "The bonemeal!"

Dorothy sighed. "I forgot," she whispered back, and turning to her mother, she said, "We'll do it together. Harry and I."

Mrs. Kane raised an eyebrow. "You'll do it together, hmm?" she said. Then she shrugged her shoulders. "Let's go, Chloe. Never look a gift horse in the mouth."

"What's a gift horse?" said Harry as he watched his mother and sister leave the room.

"Who knows?" said Dorothy, taking a plastic bag out of the closet. "Maybe it means we'll be working

13

like horses," she said, holding the bag open with two hands.

Harry picked the chicken bones off the plates and dropped them into the bag. "I thought Mom always said she was working like a dog," he said.

"Whatever," said Dorothy, securing a twisty around the bag. "Just remember. If you kill off Mom's new plants, it's all your fault, not mine."

"Neighhhhh," said Harry.

Harry put on his jacket and opened the sliding doors to the backyard. His mother was resting in her bedroom, with her feet up on a pillow. Dorothy was drawing princess pictures in her room, and Chloe was clipping an article out of the newspaper for current events.

It was dark outside, and Harry felt his way across the lawn, feeling with his foot for the large tree stump that he liked to balance on in the daytime. Farther on, he could feel the scrubby grass change to hardened soil as he reached the back of the garden.

There was a growling sound, and Harry stiffened

in his tracks. A bear? he thought. A raccoon? Then he heard the jingling of chains, and he realized that his neighbor's dog was getting some air in the yard next to them.

"Hi, Snapple," whispered Harry. He thought he heard the swishing of a tail and Snapple's happy panting, but he couldn't be sure.

Harry felt on the ground for Personality's turtle tank, hoping that a slug or a snake wouldn't find him first. At last, he touched cold smooth glass. Setting the bag of chicken bones next to him, he took a toy shovel out of his jacket pocket. He dug at the compost in the bottom of the tank, scraping and gouging at the soil. It was as hard as a rock. Sighing, Harry left the tank and found his way back into the house, chicken-bone bag in hand.

He entered the living room and knelt beside his mother's largest plant. It was leafy and green and flowerless. A cardboard picture stuck into the soil showed pretty pink flowers that the baby would love. Harry removed a large chicken bone, the leg, he thought, and stuck it into the soil. Then he picked out another, and another, and another, and poked them into the soil until the dirt was a field of chicken-bone trees. Harry wiped his hands on his pants and surveyed his work. He was tired. He'd worked hard, like a dog or a horse or whatever worked harder. Perhaps by morning, the bonemeal would produce pink flowers, in time for the baby.

In the morning, Harry woke up to the sound of his mother calling, "Harry Kane, get in here this minute!" It didn't sound like pink flowers were blooming. It didn't sound like she appreciated his hard work. It sounded bad for Harry.

Harry shuffled slowly into the living room. His mother was standing by the largest plant, arms folded and foot tapping. "What is this?" she said, pointing to the pot with the row of bones. From where Harry was standing, they looked like little tombstones.

"That's my bonemeal," said Harry in a small voice.

"Your bonemeal," Mrs. Kane said flatly.

"A good meal for the plant, so that pink flowers will grow in time for the baby."

"In time for the baby," said Mrs. Kane.

Harry thought his mother was beginning to sound like a parrot. "I wanted to welcome the baby," said Harry quickly, "into our beautiful world."

"Into our beautiful world," said Mrs. Kane gently. She looked down at her basketball tummy. "What do you think, little boy?" she said. "Will these chicken bones, stuck into this plant, welcome you into our beautiful world?"

Harry ran over to his mother and wrapped his arms around her as far as they could go. He pressed his ear against her round stomach and listened.

"What does he say?" whispered Harry's mother.

"He says yes," whispered Harry.

2

Harry in the Doghouse

PLAYING AT HIS BEST FRIEND Benjamin's house was Harry's favorite activity in the world, next to eating vanilla fudge ice cream or riding on an airplane to Grandma Rebecca's condominium in Florida or letting his pet turtle Personality walk up his knee (but he was dead now, so that didn't count).

One sunny March afternoon, as Harry and his friend trudged up the steps to Benjamin's house, a single crocus next to the bottom step practically nodded its head at Harry and said hello. At least Harry thought so, because ever since Harry's famous compost heap, it was his secret belief that plants and flowers talked. After all, only a week after Harry had enriched Mrs. Kane's potted plant with chicken bones, pink flowers had blossomed. Mr. Kane told Harry that the only thing enriched by chicken bones was Harry's imagination, but when Harry leaned his face into the blooms to smell them, he was sure he heard the plant whisper "thank you."

So Harry wished the crocus a silent hello and followed Benjamin into the hallway, where they dumped their book bags and ran straight into the kitchen for a snack.

"Did you wipe your feet?" called Benjamin's mother from the other room.

"Your mother has X-ray vision like mine," said Harry, and both boys ran back into the hallway and stamped their sneakers on the welcome mat at the door.

"Can we bring our snacks outside?" said Benjamin as he grabbed two packets of raspberry roll-ups, which Harry had heard his mother say rotted teeth and had very little to do with fresh fruit, but maybe Mrs. Tuttle didn't read labels like Mrs. Kane did.

"You're lucky," said Harry. "My mother says these rot your teeth, so she won't buy them."

Mrs. Tuttle appeared in the doorway. "Say thank you," she said, laughing, "for the delicious snack that I've given you to rot your teeth."

"Thank you," said Harry, ripping open the wrapper.

"My mother is being sarcastic," explained Benjamin. "She doesn't really want you to rot your teeth."

Mrs. Tuttle laughed again and rumpled her son's hair. "He's right, Harry. Next time I'll give you an apple."

"It's okay," said Harry. "Since my mother is pregnant, she eats lots of ice cream and cookies, so she's rotting our teeth anyway."

"Have fun, boys," said Mrs. Tuttle, clicking her teeth together and adding, "Now I feel like I need to brush my teeth!"

Harry and Benjamin grabbed their jackets and headed for the side door. "Mrs. Tuttle?" said Harry as they followed her down the hallway.

"What, Harry?" said Benjamin's mother.

Harry looked solemn. "Don't forget to floss."

"She likes you," said Benjamin, slamming the door to peals of laughter. "She says you crack her up."

"Maria the crossing guard says I'm a pip," said Harry. "That sounds like something you spit out of an orange."

"Gross," said Benjamin, sitting on the cement steps to eat his roll-up. "Want to play hide-and-seek?" He lifted up the lid to the metal garbage can next to the porch and threw his wrapper in. "Check out the new bushes my father planted to hide the garbage cans, Harry. Do you think they need your special chicken-bone meal?"

Harry didn't give the new bushes a second glance, because he was already off and running, shouting, "I'll hide first! Start counting to fifty!"

Benjamin's yard was much better than Harry's for playing hide-and-seek. The Tuttles had lots of trees and bushes and an old doghouse, which Harry promptly crawled inside. Harry hadn't hidden there since the time he and Benjamin had jumped out at

Mrs. Tuttle when she was shaking dirt out of a rug. She had screamed almost as loudly as Mrs. Kane had the day she'd found Personality dead in the dryer, only Mrs. Tuttle had accused them of giving her a heart attack. Benjamin had explained at the time that she wasn't really having a heart attack, she was sort of joking in a mad way, and Harry had understood, because Mrs. Kane often complained that he was giving her a nervous breakdown, whatever that was, and nothing ever broke as far as he could tell.

Harry scrunched up inside the little house. He didn't mind the musty smell of Benjamin's dog Arnie, who had died of old age almost two years back. Benjamin had taped a poster of dogs on the wall so Arnie wouldn't be lonely in a neighborhood full of cats.

Harry stopped studying the poster, because he caught a flash of sneakers walking past the opening. He waited quietly. Then the flash appeared again, stopping directly outside, and Benjamin stuck his face in the doorway, yelling, "Gotcha!"

Harry scrambled outside and covered his eyes.

"One, two, three, four, five . . ." he started counting to the sounds of Benjamin's running feet. Harry strained his ears to hear in which direction they were heading, and at the number fifty, took off for the side of the house, remembering the slanting cellar doors that were nice to hide under. Before he could check to see if they were locked, Harry heard a surprising "gotcha!"

Ivan Seeger stood guard over a large bush that Benjamin crawled out from under. Harry's heart sank at the sight of Ivan the Terrible (that had been Harry's nickname for Ivan from the time that he gave Harry salt instead of sugar to put in his chocolate chip cookies). Mr. Kane had told him that Ivan the Terrible was the first czar of Russia and that the name suited Ivan very well.

"I'm it," said Ivan in his usual bossy manner.

"Hide-and-seek is no fun with too many people," said Harry, recalling that Ivan had thrown crab apples at him the time he'd found Harry hiding up in a tree. "Let's play tag instead."

"You're it," said Ivan, streaking away from Harry with Benjamin following. Harry sighed and stroked a honeysuckle bush. "Get Ivan," the bush told him, and Harry took a deep breath and headed the other way, past the front of the house, around the other side, up the side steps, and straight onto the garbage can. He could see Ivan now, a few yards away, sticking out his tongue at him, saying, "Nyah, nyah, nyah!" and Harry took a flying leap at him, a flying leap right into Mr. Tuttle's new thorny bushes whose branches blended into the soil because they were the very same color. As Harry's leg met the sharpest branch, he tried to remember the scientific word for it, when an insect like a praying mantis couldn't be seen because it looked just like a stick.

Harry lay on the ground and touched his leg. It felt wet and muddy, and there was a throbbing just under the knee. He heard two pairs of feet running toward him, then Ivan shouting, "He's bleeding!" and Benjamin calling, "Maaaaa!" as he thumped up the porch steps.

Camouflage, Harry remembered as he sat up to examine the bloodied leg of his new trousers that just that morning he'd begged his mother to let him wear. They were green leafy pants with a tropical design good for blending into the jungle, camouflage pants that he had told his mother reminded him of spring. His mother had sighed deeply and said, "You can wear them, but please don't ruin them," and now she would be mad and maybe tell him that money didn't grow on trees, even camouflaged trees. The throbbing was getting worse now, and the blood was dripping down his leg, and Harry thought it would have made an interesting science experiment if it hadn't been his own leg. Harry felt like crying.

Mrs. Tuttle and Mrs. Seeger were talking in low voices above him, and Mrs. Tuttle ran away and came back with pinking shears and cut a zigzag up his pants leg. Maybe his mother would be mad at Benjamin's mother now, thought Harry, a tear rolling down his cheek.

"He's crying, Ma," said Ivan the Terrible.

"You'll be fine, Harry," said Mrs. Seeger, but her mouth looked a little twisted, and Harry wasn't convinced.

"It's deep," said Mrs. Tuttle, looking very white in the face.

Mrs. Seeger said grimly, "The emergency room."

"I can't take him," said Mrs. Tuttle. "My car is in the shop."

Mrs. Seeger, the very same mother who hadn't believed Harry when he'd told her that Ivan had put salt in his cookies, twisted her mouth the other way. "I guess I'll have to take him," she said. "Call his mother and tell her she can meet us there."

She was bossy, like Ivan.

Harry stood up. He felt dazed and a little wobbly, and he let Mrs. Seeger take his hand and lead him to the car. "Get the beach towel," she told Ivan.

"Are we going swimming first?" asked Harry, confused.

"Of course not," said Mrs. Seeger sharply. "I don't want my whole car to get bloody."

"Blood doesn't wash out," said Ivan importantly as he watched his mother spread the beach towel on the backseat. "I'll sit next to him and make sure his leg doesn't drip on the car seat."

"Thank you, honey," said Mrs. Seeger, wrapping

what looked like a dish towel around Harry's leg. "Hold this here," she instructed him.

Harry's heart sank. Now his mother would have to pay Ivan's mother for two towels *and* throw his brand-new camouflage pants into the garbage can. Harry was in trouble.

Mrs. Seeger started the engine.

"You don't get car sick, do you?" said Ivan, patting Harry's good leg. "You're not going to throw up, are you?"

Harry hadn't thought about it, but he was still feeling woozy, and his leg felt stiff. "I don't think so," he said, rolling down the window just in case.

"Throw-up doesn't stain like blood," said Ivan.

"Heavens," said Mrs. Seeger, speeding up the car as Harry gulped in deep breaths of air.

At last they pulled up to a large building. "Deepside Hospital," Harry read.

"Deep Cut Hospital, it should be called," said Ivan.

It was a pretty good joke for Ivan, but Harry didn't feel like laughing.

"Where's your mother?" muttered Mrs. Seeger as she swung open Harry's car door and helped him out.

Mrs. Kane was nowhere to be seen in the busy waiting room. "Stay here," Mrs. Seeger said to Harry. "Honey, come with Mommy," she said to Ivan. Harry thought that it was lucky for Ivan that his mother liked him, because Harry certainly didn't. Mrs. Seeger returned with some forms to fill out, but Harry only knew his address and telephone number. He had no idea what insurance was, even though Ivan recited something he called his Social Security number.

"Has he had his tetanus shot?" said a lady wearing a white cap.

"Yes!" said Harry, because he didn't want another one.

"We'll ask his mother when she comes," said Mrs. Seeger, ignoring him.

Ivan said loudly, "He'll probably need to get a needle, won't he, Ma?"

"We'll see," said Mrs. Seeger, patting her son's head.

Harry felt as though he needed his head patted, too, but his mother wasn't there and his sisters weren't there, and tears welled up in his eyes once more.

"He's crying again, Ma," said Ivan.

"I am not!" said Harry, wiping his shirt sleeve across his eyes.

Mrs. Seeger smiled at him, but it wasn't a Grandma Rebecca smile or an Aunt Sarah smile, or even an "I'm proud of you, son" smile like his father gave him when they took off the training wheels on his bicycle. It was more like a substitute teacher smile, when the teacher has no idea who you are as she waves good-bye at the end of the day.

"Harry Kane," called the lady with the cap, pushing a wheelchair over to Harry, who was waving his hand in the air.

"Hop in, young man," she said with a grin. "We'll go for a ride."

Harry felt important as he rolled down the hallway, followed by Ivan and his mother, who had to walk. He almost forgot about the needle, until he was helped onto a long white table and he lay down and stared at a sparkling light on the ceiling. He felt something cold on his leg, and it began to sting.

"Hello, Harry," said a man in white, who had bright blue eyes like Grandpa Leon's and a smile that was much nicer than Ivan the Terrible's mother's smile.

"My name is Dr. Olaf," he said, taking Harry's hand, "but my friends call me Arney. You've got a nice little jagged cut there."

"A bush did it," said Harry, wondering why Dr. Olaf was looking at the palm of his hand instead of his bloody leg. "Benjamin's dog was named Arnie, before he died. I was hiding in his doghouse before I jumped onto the garbage can and into the bush. I'm not going to get a needle, am I, Arnie?"

Dr. Olaf laughed. "I'm reading your palm, and it says that you're going to get some stitches, but you have a long life line, and you'll be outside playing in a week or two."

"But he's getting a needle, isn't he?" piped up Ivan.

Dr. Olaf whispered something in Mrs. Seeger's ear. Harry was glad when he ushered both of them out of the room, until Ivan the Terrible called from the doorway, "They're going to stitch you up with a sewing needle!"

"Is it true?" said Harry, a whooshing feeling going through his stomach as if he was riding on a roller coaster, only he wasn't having any fun at all.

"After this, you won't feel a thing," said Arney, pricking him with something. "Remember, you'll be playing ball in a week."

"Ouch," said Harry, thinking that maybe the dirt on his hands made the doctor read his palm all wrong and that really he would be limping with a cane like Great-Grandma Fanny for the rest of his life.

"Now you won't feel a thing," Arney repeated softly.

Harry raised his head and saw the doctor holding a curved needle, just like Ivan had said. It would be awful if Ivan was right and the doctor was wrong. Harry squeezed his eyes shut and waited. But Arney wasn't lying, because when Harry opened up one eye and peeked, he could see Arney sewing, in and out like he was mending a shirt with a rip in it, only Harry's leg was the ripped shirt and he didn't feel a thing.

"I think Arnie is a lucky name," said Harry, feeling much more cheerful. "A smart name. People named Arnie are smart and tell the truth. Benjamin's dog, Arnie, was smart, too."

Dr. Olaf laughed. "But I bet his name was spelled differently. Mine's A-R-N-E-Y. It means eagle in Norwegian."

"Eagle?" said Harry brightly. "I met an eagle named King once. And my sister Chloe has a nose like an eagle's. Aqua-something. We looked it up in the dictionary, and it means hooked, like an eagle. I knew it was a lucky name, because eagles are the smartest birds in the whole world."

The nurse appeared and said to Harry, "Is your mother's name Lillian Kane, and is she having a baby?"

"Yes!" said Harry excitedly, and he started to wriggle until Arney told him that he'd better lie still or he'd sew two of his toes together by mistake.

"Your Aunt Sarah brought her in," the nurse

continued. "His aunt will be here in a minute, Dr. Olaf."

"Thank you," said Arney, wrapping a bandage around Harry's leg. "You have twelve stitches, young man. You were very brave."

Aunt Sarah poked her head around the corner, looking red in the face and so much like his mother that Harry almost started to cry. But stitches were kind of exciting, and twelve was the same as a dozen, and he said to his aunt, "I have a dozen stitches, Aunt Sarah, and Arney says I was very brave, and his name means eagle so I was brave like an eagle! Where's my mother?"

"Hi, sweetheart," she said, dabbing at her forehead with a tissue. "Benjamin's mother called just as I was taking your mother to the hospital. The baby's on its way." She peered at Harry's bloody pants and made a face.

"Where is she?" said Harry. "I have to show her my stitches."

"Keep them clean and dry," said Dr. Olaf, handing Aunt Sarah a piece of paper. "Here are your instructions for follow-up care."

"She's here," said Aunt Sarah, "in another part of the hospital."

"Let's go," said Harry, swinging his legs off the table.

"Take it easy," said the doctor, winking at Aunt Sarah. "Don't go flying out of here!"

"Like an eagle!" said Harry as he took Aunt Sarah's hand. She thanked Dr. Olaf and led him out of the room and down a long corridor, straight into an elevator where she pressed a button. They stepped out onto the fourth floor. "Here's the waiting room," whispered Aunt Sarah. "Sit down and rest your leg."

"Why are we whispering?" whispered Harry as he sat down on an orange vinyl seat that squeaked.

"I don't know," said Aunt Sarah, laughing. "I guess I'm excited because your mother is having the baby!"

"Right now?" said Harry.

"Right now," said Aunt Sarah. "I was afraid she'd have it in the car!"

"Ivan's mother made me sit on a beach towel in

the car," said Harry. "Did Mama sit on a beach towel, too?"

Before she could answer, a nurse appeared. "You're Lillian Kane's sister?" she said to Aunt Sarah.

Aunt Sarah nodded and the nurse said, "It's a boy!"

"Does he look like me?" said Harry.

"As a matter of fact he does," said the nurse, pinching his cheek. "He has fat round cheeks, just like yours."

Harry decided that his first job as a big brother would have to be stopping people from pinching his little brother's cheeks. He rubbed the pinched spot and said, "Can I see my mother now?"

"In a little while," said the nurse.

While they waited, Harry told Aunt Sarah all about his stitches. Just as he was about to unwrap his bandage to show her how gross it was, the nurse came back. "You can see your baby brother now," she said, handing Aunt Sarah two green robes and matching slippers. "Put these on."

"Maybe I can dress like a doctor on Halloween," said Harry as his aunt helped him get dressed. "I can make believe I'm Arney."

Mrs. Kane was smiling when Harry walked into the room. It was a bigger, sweeter smile than Mr. Kane's when he was proud, or even Grandma Rebecca's when she was reading a birthday card that Harry had made especially for her.

"Come and meet your brother," she said to Harry, tipping a little blue bundle toward him.

Harry looked at the bundle. The nurse was right about the cheeks . . . they were very round and pink, like Harry's. But the rest of him looked more like Grandpa Leon, all red and wrinkled, with a smooth round head that didn't have a single hair growing on it.

"He's bald," whispered Harry. "I have just the right name for him."

"What name is that?" said Mrs. Kane, kissing the top of Harry's head.

"Arney," said Harry. "It's Norwegian, and it means eagle, like the bald eagle, our national emblem, and eagles are the smartest birds in the world, and Arney was my doctor, and he says I'll be playing ball in a week, and it didn't even hurt, even though I was bleeding all over Ivan the Terrible's beach towel."

"Arnie?" said Mrs. Kane, looking worried. "Isn't that the name of Benjamin's dog that died?"

"Benjamin's dog wasn't Norwegian," explained Harry. "This Arney is spelled A-R-N-E-Y, the Norwegian way. It's the perfect name."

"Arney?" repeated Mrs. Kane as she touched Harry's round cheek. "And that's the name you want?"

"Arney," said Harry, snuggling against his mother.

"How about Michael Arney Kane?" said Harry's mother, ignoring Aunt Sarah's smirk.

"Arney Michael Kane," said Harry. "As smart as an eagle."

3

The Eagle Has Landed

AUNT SARAH TOOK Harry home while his mother rested. She marched him straight into the bathroom and tried to clean him with a washcloth, but Harry wriggled away.

"I'm not the baby," he protested. "He's in the hospital, and his name is Arney Michael Kane!"

"Then you'd better do it yourself," said Aunt Sarah, handing Harry the washcloth. "I will not take you back to the hospital with a dirty face and filthy hands!"

Harry held the washcloth under running water and dabbed gently at his face. Aunt Sarah had her nose in the air and her hands on her hips, looking just like his mother when she wasn't too pleased with him. Harry scrubbed harder.

"Now brush your teeth," said Aunt Sarah.

"I didn't eat anything!" said Harry, but his aunt loomed over him and Harry took his toothbrush out of the holder. "Soon there will be one more toothbrush!" he said, squeezing a line of toothpaste onto his brush. "Arney can have my old one because I could use a new one."

"He has to grow teeth first," said Aunt Sarah. "And I think he'd like a new one of his own, don't you?"

Harry shrugged. "Well, then I'll show him how to brush the right way. Up and down, not across."

"I'm sure he would like that, Harry. Now let's find you some clean clothes." Aunt Sarah rummaged through Harry's dresser and pulled out a pair of red pants. "Are these okay?" she said.

Harry considered the pants. "Scientifically," he said, "red is good. Mama says that babies like bright colors. And I'll wear my purple Batman shirt. Arney will like Batman."

"Purple and red?" said Aunt Sarah doubtfully.

"Perfect," said Harry, slipping the shirt over his head.

A very colorful Harry walked into his mother's hospital room, wearing his red trousers, his purple Batman shirt, orange-and-white Halloween socks and yellow high-top sneakers.

"Harry!" said his mother. "How . . . bright you are! But why are you wearing your pajama top?"

"Harry Kane!" Aunt Sarah had her hands on her hips again.

"It's for Arney!" Harry said hastily. "I wanted to welcome him into this world with my favorite shirt and lots of nice colors. Maybe Dorothy will wear her Wizard of Oz shirt!"

"I'm sure the baby would love that," said Mrs. Kane, smiling as she picked at her supper. "But Daddy is bringing the girls straight from Mrs. Peet's house."

Harry examined his mother's plate full of food. "Do you like your mashed potatoes?" he said.

"You have them, honey." His mother pushed the tray toward him. "Eat what you like."

Harry ate most of his mother's supper, including the mashed potatoes (which his mother hardly ever made at home) and the tapioca pudding (which Chloe and Dorothy refused to eat because of the tiny little lumps that rolled around in their mouths). Then Aunt Sarah and Harry escorted Mrs. Kane into the corridor to look at Arney in the nursery.

"Why is he crying?" said Harry. "He's not supposed to be crying. He's supposed to be happy to see me!"

"He's brand-new, honey," said his mother.

"Maybe he's scared," said Harry, dancing a little jig for his brother outside the nursery window.

Arney continued wailing. Harry started singing "You Are My Sunshine" very loudly, until his mother shushed him because so many people were looking.

Harry turned his attention to the other babies. He counted six crying babies, including Arney, three sleeping babies, and three happy babies who were waving their little hands and feet. Then he and Aunt Sarah added them all together.

"There are twelve babies in all," Harry told his mother as they peered through the glass window.

"How many of them are crying?" said Mrs. Kane, smiling.

"Six," said Harry.

"And six and six makes twelve, right?"

"Right," said Harry. "Scientifically speaking, half of them are crying."

"Scientifically speaking," said Mrs. Kane, "half of them are not!"

"And that one," said Harry, pointing to one of the three happy babies in a pink bassinette, "is a giant!" He strained his eyes to read the name. "Hill," he said. "Hill something."

"It's Hillary. Ten pounds seven ounces," his mother read.

Harry screwed up his eyes. "Ten pounds seven ounces? How big was Arney?"

"Seven pounds four ounces. But he arrived a little early," said his mother.

"How much bigger is what's-her-name?"

"Hillary is three pounds and three ounces bigger," said Mrs. Kane.

"Hillary!" scoffed Harry. "She's no hill, she's a mountain! They could call her Hulk for short!"

Aunt Sarah started to laugh, but Mrs. Kane gave her the same look that she'd given Harry the time he'd told her that her legs jiggled when she walked. It was a look that shut you up fast. Then she turned to Harry and said sharply, "How would you like it if you heard someone call our baby a little shrimp because he was so small?"

"I wouldn't mind," said Harry, waving at Arney, who was still crying. "Maybe he wants to be with us again. Maybe he's crying because he wants to get away from Hillary the Hulk."

"Her mother or father could be standing right next to us," Harry's mother bent and spoke softly in his ear. "Stop that right now!"

Harry shrugged his shoulders and turned to look at the man standing next to him. He had white hair and a face with more wrinkles and brown spots than Grandpa Leon had. Harry watched carefully, but he couldn't figure out which baby the old man was looking at.

"I don't think he's Hillary's father," whispered

Harry, but Harry's whisper sounded almost as loud as Mrs. Kane's regular way of talking. "I think he's too old. He looks more like a grandpa."

Mrs. Kane rolled her eyes, and Aunt Sarah made a snorting sound. "Don't encourage him," she said sharply to her sister, and Aunt Sarah tried to wipe the smile off her face, but Harry could tell that it was hard for her.

"Hillary has more hair than Arney," said Harry. "She's a very hairy hulk."

"Harry!" Mrs. Kane's voice was stern. "Enough! Chloe didn't have much hair, either," she added, "and look at her now." Mrs. Kane was pointing a finger down the hallway, beaming that special smile again as she watched Chloe and Dorothy walk up the hall with their long hair flowing.

Mr. Kane followed, huffing and puffing, and Harry heard him say, "The girls were so eager to get here that I almost got a ticket for speeding!" He kissed his wife quickly and murmured, "I'm sorry I wasn't here, honey."

"I was here!" said Harry, sticking his leg out

44

toward his father. "I was very brave, the doctor told me. I was the bravest patient who ever got stitches."

Mr. Kane quickly admired Harry's leg but wouldn't peek down inside the bandage to see the stitches. He was much more interested in looking through the nursery window. Chloe and Dorothy had already found the baby and pointed him out to their father.

"He's beautiful," whispered Mr. Kane. "He's the most beautiful baby in the nursery."

"Not so loud," whispered Harry. "The man next to us could be a father, even though he looks like a grandfather."

"Sorry," said Mr. Kane.

Mrs. Kane burst out laughing. "Like father, like son," she said.

At last the nurses started wheeling the babies into their mothers' rooms. Harry and his sisters sat quietly while Mrs. Kane nursed the baby.

"I think he's hungry from being in your stomach so long," said Harry.

"Look at his little fingers," said Dorothy.

"His eyelashes are longer than mine!" said Chloe.

The babies were returned to the nursery just as visiting hours began. Mrs. Kane put lipstick on, straightened the blankets on her bed, and instructed Dorothy to comb her hair. People arrived carrying bunches of floating pink and blue balloons, vases in the shape of booties filled with flowers, cannisters of hard candy, and white bakery boxes brimming with cookies and cakes. The room reminded Harry a little of the Party Palace, where he had gone for Jessica Weinstein's birthday party.

But the Party Palace had fun activities like painting ceramic statues of your favorite cartoon characters, and there was none of that in Mrs. Kane's hospital room. Harry borrowed a pencil and paper from his mother and drew pictures for a while, but nobody looked at them. Everyone was too busy giving presents to the four mothers and filing back out into the hallway to admire the babies in the nursery. Not a single person paid any attention to Harry's bandaged leg.

When Grandpa Leon and Grandma Rebecca arrived, Grandma waved him away. "Let me just go take a look at my new grandson, Harry. Then I'll have a good look at your boo-boo."

Harry was not happy. Boo-boo! He certainly didn't have a boo-boo, and he hadn't used that silly word for at least two years.

"It's a wound," said Harry, tipping his nose in the air. But Grandma didn't hear a word. She was already rushing out of the room to find Arney.

When Aunt Laura arrived, Harry was sure she would prefer her nephew's bandaged leg to a newborn baby. Aunt Laura was his mother's unmarried sister and had told Harry many times that he was her favorite nephew. But she patted him absentmindedly on the head and was as goo-goo eyed as the rest of them.

Uncle Peter walked into the hospital room, and Harry stuck his leg out in front of him like a ballet dancer. His uncle just skirted around it without a glance. He went straight over to Aunt Sarah, put his arm around her, and said, "Someday this will be us, honey." Aunt Sarah said, "I hope so," and they started talking to Harry's mother about having babies and never stopped, even when Harry invited

Uncle Peter to look at his stitches. Harry couldn't believe it. After all, Uncle Peter had made Harry look at his old football scars from college plenty of times.

Harry sat on a chair in the corner by his mother's bed and moped, but moping is a complete waste of energy if nobody notices.

"I'm bored," he said to a thorny little cactus on the windowsill. Harry was certain that he heard the prickly plant mutter, "Bug off."

A boy about Harry's size stood next to him. "Do you mind if I share this corner with you?" he said. "I'm sick of babies."

Harry patted the edge of his seat and said, "Watch out for the cactus. He's in a bad mood." The boy didn't call Harry a fruitcake like Ivan the Terrible had on the day he'd caught Harry saying hello to his teacher's African violet. He just nodded and gave Harry a truck. Then they stood by the windowsill driving their trucks in between little white baby shoes, using a giant greeting card that Grandma Rebecca and Grandpa Leon had brought. The part that said CONGRATULATIONS ON YOUR

BUNDLE OF JOY! made a great tunnel. They came to a screeching halt in front of a champagne bottle full of jelly beans, ate a few, revved up their cars, sped past a line of baby bottles, and parked on a bib with a picture of a car on it.

Then Harry the Scientist had an idea for a science experiment. Harry and his new friend floated different-colored jelly beans in Mrs. Kane's pitcher of water, and Harry observed that the pink ones turned white. They were just beginning to test the black jelly beans when Chloe came over.

"Leave those jelly beans alone!" she yelled.

"It's an experiment," Harry protested.

"We could do it with my bag of M&Ms next," said Harry's new friend excitedly.

"Do whatever you want to your M&Ms," Chloe said snootily, "but leave my pink jelly beans alone, because they're bubble-gum flavor, and that's my favorite, and I know for a fact that Dorothy loves the black ones." She called across her mother's bed to her sister. "Don't you like the black jelly beans, Dorothy? Harry is ruining them."

Dorothy was sitting next to her mother, feeding

her newborn baby doll. She stopped long enough to yell at Harry, "You know very well that I love licorice, so leave the black ones alone!"

Harry sighed and started picking out the black and pink jelly beans. "It's a good thing my mother didn't have another girl," he said to his friend. "Two sisters are enough!" He stuck his leg out. "They won't even look at my stitches!"

"Cool! Stitches!" said the boy. "What did you do to get them?"

"I landed on a bush when we were playing tag," said Harry, pulling the edge of the bandage away from his leg so the boy could peek underneath. "Can you see some of the stitches? I have a dozen!"

"Cool!" the boy repeated so loudly that Dorothy put down her baby doll and came over to see what she was missing.

"Oh, gross!" she squealed when she peered inside the bandage. "It looks like it should be in a horror movie! Next time you should watch where you're jumping!"

Harry said that if Mr. Tuttle had borrowed some

of his special bonemeal, maybe the bushes would have grown enough leaves so that Harry could see them. "They were camouflaged," he explained to his friend.

"Harry thinks that plants and flowers talk to him," said Dorothy.

"They do!" said Harry.

"It's possible," said the boy, defending Harry. "They're living things." Then he turned to Harry and said in a serious voice, "It's just too bad the bushes didn't warn you ahead of time!"

Harry thought about it for a moment and said, "You know, you're right." Then they both started laughing so loudly that the woman in the bed across from Mrs. Kane called out, "Jared! Stop cackling!"

"She's in a bad mood," Jared told Harry. "The baby was so big that they had to cut my mother's stomach to get her out. That's called a C-section."

Harry was impressed. "My mother's stomach looked like a basketball," he said, "except I don't think they cut it. But I was the first one in the family to see the baby!"

"Chloe saw him first, when they went for Mama's test," said Dorothy, popping a black jelly bean into her mouth.

"That was a photograph of him inside her belly," said Harry hotly. "I was the first one to see him outside. And he gets to share my room with me, so I'm lucky he's a boy."

Dorothy looked hurt. "You liked it when I shared a room with you, Harry. You cried when we moved into the new house."

Jared spoke up before Harry could answer. "I'm glad my baby's a girl," he said. "This way she won't mess with my Nintendo and my trucks."

Dorothy said, "Who says girls don't like Nintendo and trucks?" She grabbed hold of Jared's yellow pickup truck and ran it up his leg. "I could make a whole play about a little girl who runs away with this truck."

Harry nodded. "Dorothy's right," he said. "I know a lot about sisters that I could teach you."

"I think my baby is going to be the best sister ever," said Jared. "But maybe you could come over to my house and we could test out the M&Ms."

Harry's father called him. "Can we see you for a moment, Harry?" He motioned for him to stand next to Dorothy and Chloe as they gathered around Mrs. Kane's bed.

"We need a family conference about the name," said Mr. Kane.

"His name is Arney," said Harry. "It means eagle, in Norwegian."

"Yuck," said Chloe. "It sounds like that dinosaur."

"That's Barney," said Harry. "Barney doesn't mean eagle in Norwegian."

"I thought we chose Michael," said Chloe. "I thought Dad wanted Dakota but we didn't want a name that sounded like a cowboy, so we chose Michael, with Mickey for short."

Dorothy spoke up. "We have a Michael in my class who puts crayon wrappers and staples in his mouth," she said.

"Staples?" said Mrs. Kane, horrified.

"But he spits them out right away," said Dorothy.

Harry chimed in. "We have a Mickey in my class who picks his nose and—"

"Harry!" warned Mr. Kane. "Arney Michael Kane," he said. "Let me try it out."

"Michael Arney Kane," said Harry's mother.

"Arney!" called Dorothy loudly.

"Arney," said Chloe softly.

"It's really perfect," pleaded Harry. "My doctor saved my life today, and his name was Arney, and that's a lucky sign. Don't you want the baby to be lucky?"

"Does it really mean eagle?" said Dorothy.

"It does," said Harry.

"If I can't get used to it," said Chloe, "I'm going to give him a nickname."

"Just don't call him Hulk, like Harry called that big baby in the nursery," said Mrs. Kane.

"She was huge!" said Harry.

Jared called good-bye as he followed his father out of the room. "Tell your mom to get my phone number from my mom," he said. "Then you can come over."

"Can I go over to Jared's house to visit him and his new baby?" said Harry to his mother.

"I'm sure you can," said Mrs. Kane. "Do you like your new baby brother?" she said to Jared.

"My sister," said Jared. "And her name is Hillary."

"Hillary?" said Harry, dumbstruck.

Jared smiled and said proudly, "She's the biggest one in the nursery!"

"No kidding!" said Harry, looking at his mother. "Our baby's name is Arney, but he's not quite as big."

"That's okay," said Jared. "He's big enough." Jared waved his hand and left.

"His baby's name was Hillary?" said Mrs. Kane.

"The Hulk," whispered Harry.

"She's big," said Chloe.

"Very big," said Dorothy.

"Big and quiet," said Harry, "and kind of cute," because his new friend was Jared, and Hillary was Jared's sister, and Jared believed that Harry really did talk to plants and had liked making jelly-bean experiments and had let him borrow his truck. Maybe Jared would let Harry observe his quiet baby sister and figure out how to make Arney stop crying, scientifically.

"Arney," said Chloe.

"Arney and Hillary," said Dorothy. "Maybe they'll be friends someday. They have the same birthday."

"The Eagle and the Hulk," said Harry, stroking his chin as he imagined a scientist might. "Could be."

4

Harry the Discoverer

HARRY LIKED the springtime, because springtime was the season of discovery. A crocus sprouting overnight was a major find for Harry on his morning walk to Walnut School. April showers brought a lot more than May flowers. He stopped to pry a rock loose from the soggy earth and made a second discovery: the bugs and beetles were out again.

"Maybe if I take a beetle to school, I can identify it in science class," said Harry, searching in his book bag for his lunch box so that he could empty it and use it.

"Don't you dare, Harry," said Chloe, who

thought she was the big boss because she was in the fourth grade. "You'll have to wait until you can get a jar with holes in it. I'm in charge since Mom can't walk us, and I say no."

"I'm second in charge," said Dorothy, a look of horror on her face. "Mom definitely wouldn't let you put beetles in your lunch box."

Harry scowled. "Mama's so busy making goo-goo noises over Arney, she wouldn't even notice," he said. Harry put his hands on his hips. "I'll bet Albert Einstein's mother didn't forget all about him when she had a new baby. I'll bet she helped him collect bugs. I'll bet she studied them with him." Mrs. Ott had told the class all about the famous physicist who had received the 1921 Nobel Prize in physics. Even though Harry was still not sure what physics was, he was certain of one thing. Albert Einstein liked making discoveries, too.

Chloe was never at a loss for an answer. "He didn't study bugs," she said. "He was good in math. Now walk, Harry, or we'll be late for school."

"And my teacher says he didn't talk until he was three," said Dorothy, prodding Harry into motion.

"So he probably didn't bother his sisters half as much as you do."

Harry mumbled something as he waited for Maria the crossing guard to escort him across the street.

"Cat got your tongue, Harry?" she said, pinching his cheek.

Harry rubbed his face and said, "My brother Arney has cheeks like mine, and he told me that he doesn't like when people pinch them."

Maria winked at Dorothy and said, "Just a month old, and he's talking already? My son Michael didn't talk until he was two."

Harry warmed to the subject. "My mother says he's a bigger genius than Albert Einstein. Albert Einstein waited until he was three to talk, and Arney talks already."

Dorothy grabbed hold of her brother's arm. "Don't go telling fibs, Harry," she said in his ear.

"Well, he talks to me," said Harry, running into the school yard to look for Benjamin. Unlike his sisters, Benjamin didn't mind a little fib here and there.

Harry joined his friend, who was doing a stomping dance on the biggest puddle in the school yard. His mother wouldn't like it, but it felt good not to worry about getting his bandage wet since the doctor had recently taken out the stitches.

The bell rang, and Harry followed Benjamin into school. He was looking forward to science class, which came right after their reading groups on Friday mornings. Maybe next week Mr. Gezzik would let him bring a jarful of beetles into the classroom, and he could help Harry identify them.

Mr. Gezzik had other ideas. He was more interested in animals than insects—mammals, to be exact. He talked about some of the features that make mammals different from other animals. On the blackboard, he wrote, "Mammals are the only animals that have hair."

Harry raised his hand. "What about a whale?" he said. "A whale is a mammal, and I've never seen a hairy whale."

"In fact," said Mr. Gezzik, "they have a few hairs. Not many, but a few."

"Like Grandpa Leon and my new baby," said

Harry to no one in particular, but everybody laughed.

Next, Mr. Gezzik wrote down "sweat glands."

Jessica Weinstein raised her hand. "My parakeet flies around my house a lot. You mean she doesn't sweat?"

"No, she doesn't," said Mr. Gezzik.

"My father sweats a lot," said Mario. Mario's father had more muscles than Mr. Kane, and when he jump-roped in gym class for the children, he looked like a boxer getting ready for a fight. When Harry had told his father how strong Mr. Enzo was, Mr. Kane said, "Postmen use different muscles."

Harry raised his hand and said, "King, the bald eagle we met last year, could pluck chickens and take the heads off fish without sweating. I guess he couldn't sweat because birds don't have sweat glands. And King had beautiful feathers, which mammals don't have, right, Mr. Gezzik?"

"Right," said the teacher, writing "no feathers" on the board. Directly underneath, he wrote the words "mammary glands," and read them out loud.

Ivan raised his hand and called out, "That must

have something to do with the mother! Mammary. Mama. Get it?"

"As a matter of fact, it does," said Mr. Gezzik, laughing. "Mammary glands supply the young with milk, and they are only found in mammals. You know how a human mother nurses a baby. Well, in most animals the mammary glands are in two rows running along the sides of the stomach. They're called the milk lines."

"My mother has a milk line," said Harry. "From my house to the supermarket where we buy our milk!" The class laughed loudly, and Harry beamed. It was nice getting attention from everybody.

Benjamin raised his hand. "If you take the last two letters off mammary and you add an *L*, you get a mammal!"

"That's exactly right, Benjamin," said Mr. Gezzik. "We get the word "mammals" from the name of these glands." He wrote down "no eggs" and read the words out loud.

"No eggs for breakfast," yelled Harry. "They like muffins better!"

"Lay one more egg like that one, Harry," said

Mr. Gezzik, "and you'll be off to the principal's office."

Harry's smile faded a little. He listened quietly as Mr. Gezzik added that monotremes, like the spiny anteaters and the platypus, were the only mammals that laid eggs.

"Warm-blooded," wrote Mr. Gezzik.

"I want to suck your blood!" said Ivan in a voice that reminded Harry of Count Dracula.

Mr. Gezzik said quietly, "I will not have any more disruptions, boys."

Harry was not pleased. Mr. Gezzik was actually putting Harry in the same boat with Ivan the Terrible! Harry was so upset that he almost didn't hear Mr. Gezzik give the assignment.

"I want you to choose a mammal," said Mr. Gezzik. "Then, in your own words, write a few sentences about it. I'd like you to draw a picture of the animal, too."

Harry looked at the poster of mammals Mr. Gezzik had pinned on the bulletin board. Harry's mammal had to be special. It had to be scary. It had to be interesting. Then one picture caught his eye, perhaps because Ivan the Terrible had reminded him of Count Dracula. Harry knew exactly which animal he would write his very first report on—it had to be a bat.

At home after school, Harry told his sister Chloe that he was going to write his very first report on a bat. Chloe raised one eyebrow the way only a fourth grader could. "You can hardly write a sentence," she said, prying an Oreo cookie in half.

Dorothy could remember when she could hardly write a sentence, and she said, "If you need me to spell anything, just ask." She took the half of the Oreo cookie that Chloe handed her and popped it into her mouth. Chloe only ate the side with the icing on it.

Harry crammed a whole cookie into his mouth and said, "Mr. Gezzik says we can use first-grade spelling." Then he ran to the bookshelf in the living room and took out the encyclopedia marked *B*. "Read me the part about bats," he said to Dorothy, taking a bite of another cookie.

"Don't get that book dirty," said Mrs. Kane, speeding into the kitchen. Holding Arney over her shoulder, she picked up the telephone and dialed a number. "Hank? Bring home diapers and wipes. The baby has diarrhea."

Harry spit out the rest of his cookie. "Gross!" he yelled, stomping out of the room.

"I don't get it," said Dorothy.

"What?" Chloe broke a second cookie in two.

"He wants to take beetles in his lunch box, he likes making jelly beans turn terrible colors, and he gets grossed out by a word?" Dorothy shook her head.

"He's probably upset because Mom isn't giving him any attention," said Chloe.

Mrs. Kane hung up the phone. "I'm not?" she said in a small voice.

"You're not," said Chloe kindly. "Remember when I didn't like being the big sister? Well, Harry is the left-out big brother."

"When did you get so smart?" said Mrs. Kane.

"I was smart when I was born," said Chloe, picking up the telephone at the first ring. "It's Grandpa," she said to her mother. "Maybe Harry can have a special time with Grandpa."

Mrs. Kane widened her eyes and spoke into the telephone. "Dad? How would you like to have a small neglected boy to dinner? You would? Let me ask him."

Harry jumped at the idea. No sisters, no parents, no screaming Arney who really didn't talk at all, even though Harry had told Maria the crossing guard that he did. In fact, it was a great disappointment to Harry that his brother was such a dud. He cried most of the time, in spite of Harry's scientific suggestions; he made in his diaper; he bobbed his head; he drank; he slept. That was it.

Harry told Grandma and Grandpa all about it at the supper table.

"I've tried singing to him and making believe I'm Batman and dancing in front of him, and nothing makes him stop crying. I'm going to visit Jared's new baby to see why she's so quiet."

"All babies are different," said Grandma, serving Harry a heaping plateful of spaghetti. "Just you wait. When he gets a little older, he won't leave you alone!"

Harry twirled a forkful and ate it. "Dad says that

your spaghetti sauce tastes like catsup, but I like it," he said.

Grandpa coughed and dabbed at a smile with his napkin. "Your grandma's cooking is grand!" he said.

Grandma sat down at the table with a sigh.

"Don't feel bad, Grandma. Chloe and Dorothy like it, too!" Harry looked anxiously at his grandmother.

"Grandma hasn't been sleeping too well lately." Grandpa patted her hand. "Maybe tonight you'll get some sleep, Rebecca."

"I don't know what it is," said Grandma. "I wake up when I hear these funny noises."

"It's the radiator," said Grandpa.

"Maybe," said Grandma, but she didn't look convinced.

Harry chewed on a piece of bread and butter. He waited until he swallowed before speaking. "Do you snore, Grandpa?"

"He does," said Grandma, buttering Harry another piece of bread. "But that's not it."

"Sounds as bad as Arney," said Harry.

"Does Arney wake you, *tatalah?*" Grandma stroked Harry's cheek. Harry thought it was much nicer than being pinched.

"Mama says I sleep like a log." That's when Harry had an idea. He turned his mouth down at the corners. "Except for lately," he said sadly. "Lately I wake up and hear him, screaming in my ear. Then I can't get back to sleep and I'm tired at school."

"Well, tomorrow is Saturday," said Grandpa. "You can sleep late."

Harry sighed. "Arney wakes up so early," he said. "If only I had some other place to sleep."

Grandma and Grandpa started laughing. "Harry Kane," said Grandma, chucking him under the chin, "would you like to sleep at our house tonight? I'll call your mother."

"Hurray!" said Harry. "Did you make tapioca pudding?"

After Harry ate some of Grandma's tapioca pudding, Harry watched a dinosaur show with Grandma and a show about an oversized family which Grandpa said was a lot of hooey. Then Grandpa made up a bed on the couch for Harry, gave Harry a toothbrush and a fresh towel, and said good night.

Harry lay on the couch. Light from the hallway dimly lit a dresser full of framed photographs. His mother was a smiling little girl. Chloe looked grouchy in last year's school picture. Dorothy was curtseying in one of her school plays. Grandpa was hugging Grandma. Harry was pointing to a branch in a tree. It must have been taken when he'd found a nest in their backyard.

Harry was just drifting off to sleep when he heard the noise—a fluttering sound, then a scratching. But not on the floor, like Mrs. Peet's cat when she clawed the furniture. Up on the ceiling. Harry pulled down the covers and crept out of bed. His heart was hammering, and he held his breath to see if he could hear the noise again. There it was—a flapping of wings. Harry's heart leaped. Maybe it was an eagle! Harry shook his head. He had to be scientific about this discovery. He had to think like Albert Einstein.

Harry walked softly toward the light in the hall-way. The bedroom door was ajar. He peeked inside and listened. Grandpa definitely snored, but he couldn't tell if his grandmother was sleeping.

"Grandma!" Harry whispered. There was no answer. "Grandma!" Harry whispered a little louder.

"Harry?" Grandma lifted her head up from her pillow. "What's the matter?"

"I heard it, Grandma. It's not the radiator and it's not Grandpa's snoring."

Grandma sat up in bed and lifted her legs over the side. "Where are my slippers, Harry?"

Harry found them, and Grandma bent to put them on. "Now get the flashlight from the dresser drawer."

Harry found it in a second, flipped on the switch, and handed it to Grandma.

"Let's go," she said. Harry the Discoverer took Grandma the Explorer's hand, and he led her on tiptoe into the living room.

"There," said Harry, pointing to the corner of the room by the curtains. "That's where I heard the noise."

Grandma directed the beam of light up the cracked plaster to the top of the curtain rod. Suddenly, there was a fluttering of wings and a chirping sound, and Grandma dropped the flashlight with a thump.

Harry picked it up just as quickly and raised the light until he found the dark object in the corner. The chirping got louder. "I can't believe it, Grandma," said Harry. "Maybe he came to help me!"

"Who?" said Grandma, her voice quavering.

"The bat!" said Harry. "It's a brown bat, and he's making that noise to scare us away. He's trying to look ferocious, like it says in my book!"

"I'd better get Grandpa," she said, without moving an inch.

"They eat mosquitoes, Grandma, not people." Harry turned off the flashlight. "It's a good thing Dorothy helped me read the whole book."

Grandma looked down at her grandson. "How do we get him out of here?" she whispered.

"Open the windows wide, Grandma."

Grandma followed Harry's directions.

"Now turn on all the lights. Bats can see great, and the light will help him find his way out."

Grandma switched on the lights. "Now what?" she said.

"Just wait, Grandma," said Harry, his eyes examining the shape of the bat like a scientist would.

At first, Harry thought that the book might be wrong, because the bat stayed exactly where he was. Suddenly he took off, sailed around the ceiling and straight out the window.

Grandma sat down on Harry's bed. "Harry," she said, holding out her hand and pulling him toward her. "You're my hero of a grandson. I thought I was going crazy."

"I'm your scientist of a grandson," said Harry. "I make discoveries. Maybe next time I'll discover how to get my brother Arney to stop crying."

"Shall we go have a cup of tea and talk about it?" said Grandma.

Harry shook his head. "Scientists don't drink tea, Grandma. They drink hot chocolate." And Harry just happened to discover some in Grandma's kitchen cupboard.

5

George, Harry, and Booker T.

HARRY CAME HOME from school with a mission. He marched straight to his room and opened both windows wide. The cool air wafted into Harry's room. By bedtime, the room would be cold. Harry ran to the linen closet and grabbed a handful of old rags from a basket on the floor. Then he scattered them on the floor of his bedroom and shut the door. He lay down on the pile of rags and was satisfied.

At suppertime, it was hard to get a word in. Dorothy was talking about the play she'd seen in school assembly. Chloe wanted her father to drive her to the library after dinner. Mrs. Kane held a screaming Arney on her lap and tried to eat without dribbling food all over the baby.

By the time his mother took the container of frozen yogurt out of the freezer for dessert, Harry still hadn't had a chance to tell the family about Black History Month in Mrs. Ott's class. At last, there was a moment of silence as Arney sucked on a bottle and his sisters ate dessert.

"There's this little boy," began Harry, "who was born a slave. And he never even got a chance to play. He was always working."

"Sounds like me," said Mrs. Kane, shifting Arney as she tried to finish eating the rest of her macaroni.

Harry considered his mother's answer. "You're not really a slave, Mama."

"You just feel like one sometimes," said Dorothy.

Mr. Kane scooped some coffee into the coffeemaker. "I think your mother is just feeling a little overwhelmed," he said. "With the new baby and everything."

"Like I felt when Mrs. Ott gave us three pages of math and four pages of phonics for homework," said Harry.

"Just like that," said Mrs. Kane, dabbing at a blob of spaghetti sauce that had landed on the baby's sleeve. "There's nothing funny about slavery," she added. "Please go on."

Harry continued. "Well, he slept in one room with his brothers and sisters, on grain sacks on the floor, and all they had was a fireplace for cooking and heating up the house."

Chloe slid her spoon across the frozen yogurt, making it look particularly delicious, but Harry shook his head when Mr. Kane put a dish of it in front of him. If he was going to find out what it was like to live like the little boy his teacher had told them about, he couldn't eat a lot of food.

Harry pointed to the frozen yogurt. "It was freezing cold in the little cabin in the winter." Then he pointed to his father's steaming cup of fresh coffee. "And it was hot like that in the summer. Oh, I forgot the worst part. It was against the law for slaves to go to school."

"That part isn't so bad," said Chloe, who had a math test the next day.

Harry said, "I was thinking. If everybody else is

75

allowed to do it, and you're not, because of the color of your skin, it's not fair, and you wouldn't like it."

Mr. Kane said to Chloe, "How would you like it if everyone with . . . with . . . an aquiline nose wasn't allowed to go to school?"

"He means hooked, like yours," said Harry. "Like an eagle's."

"I see what you mean," said Chloe, rubbing her nose. "I'd be mad."

"And he didn't know his last name, so when he finally got to go to school, he made one up for himself."

"Oh, bother," said Mrs. Kane, dripping frozen yogurt on Arney's foot as he began to cry. "I'm sorry, Harry, but I'm going to have to go into the other room. Can you tell me more later?"

After Mrs. Kane left, Chloe and Harry cleared the dishes. Mr. Kane washed while Dorothy dried. Chloe ran to the bathroom to comb her hair, while her father tapped his foot impatiently. "Let's get to the library so I can come home and take a bath,

Chloe," he called to her. "My back has been bothering me."

"Try carrying Arney around all day," called Mrs. Kane from the couch in the living room.

"I have to write another report," Harry said to Dorothy, who had started a drawing of the play she had seen.

"On what?" said Dorothy.

"On the boy I told you about. His name is in my book bag. I think he called himself Washington."

"George Washington Carver," said Dorothy importantly. "We studied him, too. Catch Dad before he leaves, and he can get you a book about him."

Harry ran into the hallway. "Can you get me a book on George Washington Carver?" he said.

"You can get me a book on babies that won't stop crying," said Mrs. Kane miserably. She peered at Arney, who was red in the face from screaming. "This poor baby cries whenever he's not eating or sleeping."

"Was I like that?" said Harry, covering his ears as Arney turned up the volume.

"You were an angel," said Mrs. Kane, standing to do the rhythmic bobbing that she had read about in the paper. "This kind of up-and-down movement is supposed to soothe a baby."

"Not our baby," said Harry, laughing, but his mother didn't even crack a smile.

Mr. Kane took Harry's coat out of the closet. "I think you'd better come with me, Harry. I'll help you find your own book."

"Good-bye, Mama," said Harry, putting on his jacket.

"Good-bye, honey," said Mrs. Kane, rocking her way toward her bedroom.

At the library, Harry and Mr. Kane went to the section marked BIOGRAPHIES.

"Look for the Cs," said Mr. Kane, sitting down at the nearby table.

"Carver!" Harry announced triumphantly, handing his father the book.

"Good," said Mr. Kane, opening up to the first page. "Let's read this together so you can write your report."

Harry was surprised when he found out more

about George Washington Carver. He was a scientist who liked to discover things, just like Harry. He loved to learn. He liked to pick up wildflowers, weeds, and bugs, and examine them, which reminded Harry of the day he'd found the beetles that Chloe wouldn't let him put in his lunch box. Best of all, George kept a secret garden in the woods. When he was ten years old, people started calling him "the plant doctor."

Then the slaves were freed, and George heard all about a school for black children. He worked hard and learned all he could. He moved from place to place, chopping wood, washing clothes, digging ditches, and planting, all the time trying to attend school when he could. At last he went to an agricultural college. He learned about soil and manure and crossbreeding, where he put pollen from one plant onto the flower of another and produced a new kind of seed. He was the first black man to graduate from the school and become a teacher.

Harry's father looked at his watch. "Let me read you the rest, before the library closes." By the time Chloe was ready to leave, Harry had written,

"George Washinton Carver was a grate man. He was born a slave. They kept him from scool but he loved to lern. He helped the south make money from peenuts. When I grow up I'd like to be like him. He liked bugs to." Then he signed his name, "Harry Kane."

Mr. Kane read the paper. "Very good, Harry," he said, smiling. "Read it to your mother when you get home."

It was quiet in the house when they arrived. Dorothy had the television on low, and Mrs. Kane was making lunches.

"Did you write your report?" she said.

"He's a scientist!" said Harry. "I wish I could have met him." Harry took out his paper and cleared his throat, just as his brother Arney started screaming from the crib in Harry's room.

Mr. Kane appeared in the doorway. "I just ran myself a bath," he said, apologetically. "Can you go?"

Mrs. Kane sighed. "I'm sorry, Harry. Why don't you get ready for bed?"

Why don't I give Arney away? thought Harry.

He'd make a good watchdog, because he'd scare away burglars. Harry went to his room and closed the door. It smelled like baby wipes and powder. Harry shouted "Peeww!" as loudly as he could. It made him feel a little better. Then he put his report back into his knapsack, took his dinosaur pajamas out of the drawer, and put them on. He realized that he hadn't had a bath in two days. That was the only good thing about Arney. His mother just didn't have the time.

Harry got into bed and pulled the covers up to his neck. Someone had shut the windows, but the room was still freezing. Harry's stomach started grumbling, and then he remembered. He wanted to see what it felt like to be a little boy who worked all day and slept on the floor in the cold, who didn't know his last name and couldn't go to school. Harry got out of his warm bed and lay down on the pile of rags. He pulled an old towel over his body. He turned over onto his stomach, but the floor felt just as hard. He wished he'd eaten more for supper, but the little boy his teacher had told him about got even less to eat and worked in the fields all day instead of going to the library with his father. Still, all that reading and thinking had made him tired, and Harry fell asleep with his stomach growling, in his drafty room, under the towel his father had kept for rags, dreaming about peanuts and George Washington Carver.

When Harry woke up, he was in his very own bed. Someone had ruined his experiment, but he had no time to find out who, because mornings were the worst in the Kane household, ever since Arney.

Downstairs, Dorothy was battling with Mrs. Kane over what she wanted to wear to school.

"That's a summer dress," said Mrs. Kane, lips pursed. "You'll freeze to death."

"I don't care," said Dorothy, folding her arms in such a way that Harry knew she wouldn't budge.

Chloe sat transfixed in front of the television set.

"Chloe!" Mrs. Kane was inches from her eldest daughter's ear, but she didn't move. "For the fifth time, brush your teeth!"

Harry ate his waffle and went into the bathroom to brush his teeth. He spit toothpaste into the sink and rinsed his mouth with water. "Did you remember my snack?" he called to his mother. "You forgot to pack one yesterday."

Mrs. Kane stood in the doorway. She had dark circles under her eyes, and Harry thought her hair looked a little like a messy bird's nest. "I forgot," she said, jumping as she heard Dorothy shout from the living room that Arney was smelling up the whole place. "Harry," she pleaded. "Can you get an apple from the refrigerator and throw it into your knapsack?"

"Sure," said Harry, running past his mother into the kitchen, grabbing an apple and unzipping his knapsack while it was upside down so that his notebook fell on the floor. A slip of paper slid across the tile.

Harry picked it up and read it. "Oh, no!" he wailed. "It can't be! My life is ruined!"

"What?" said Mrs. Kane, running into the kitchen with a naked Arney under one arm.

"What?" said Dorothy, slipping a sweater over her summer dress as she ran into the room.

"What happened?" called Chloe from the living room as she switched off the television set.

"It says Booker T. Washington on the paper," said Harry miserably.

"So?" said his mother. "You did your report last night." Arney wriggled in her arms. "Chloe, bring me a diaper, quick."

Harry glared at his mother. "That's all you can say?" he shouted. " 'Bring me a diaper, quick?' "

"Harry," said his mother, laying the baby on the kitchen table and expertly fastening a diaper around him. "What's the trouble?"

"I did my report on George Washington Carver, not Booker T. Washington, and it's his fault," shouted Harry, pointing to Arney, who had his hand on Harry's sticky waffle plate.

"Oh, my goodness," said Mrs. Kane, sitting down with a thump as she pulled Arney off the table. "I'm sorry, Harry. Don't you think Mrs. Ott will understand?" She wiped Arney's hand with a napkin.

"Humph," said Harry, jamming his notebook back into his knapsack and putting on his jacket. Chloe and Dorothy were quiet as they put on their coats and opened the front door.

"See you after school," called Mrs. Kane as they walked down the steps. "I'm sorry, Harry!"

Mrs. Kane walked back into the kitchen and noticed the lone apple sitting on the kitchen table. She scooped it up and ran to the door. "You forgot your apple!" she shouted, but Harry was long gone.

When Harry read his paper out loud in front of the class, he said, "My brother Arney messed everything up, and that's why I wrote this report on George Washington Carver instead of Booker T. Washington. But I still want to be like him when I grow up." Then Harry sat down. He stood up again. "I mean I want to be like George Washington Carver, not my crummy brother Arney."

Mrs. Ott smiled. "George Washington Carver and Booker T. Washington had some things in common," she said. "Let's try to name a few of them."

Ivan raised his hand. "They were both black," he said.

"That's true," said Mrs. Ott. "What else?"

Harry said, "They were both slaves when they were born."

Jessica waved her hand in the air. "They were both great men," she said.

"Good," said the teacher. "In fact, George Washington Carver was invited by Dr. Washington to teach agriculture at his school in Tuskegee, Alabama."

"I know, I know," said Harry excitedly. "They weren't allowed to go to school when they were slaves, but they went anyway. They loved to learn!"

"Very good, Harry," said Mrs. Ott. "Booker T. Washington believed in learning by doing. And so did George Washington Carver. Carver started a school for farmers. He showed them how to feed their cows so the cows would give more milk. He taught them how to make compost heaps and fertilizer so that the fruits and vegetables would grow better. He found new ways for people to use peanuts, like peanut oil and peanut butter, and even cream for ladies' faces made out of peanuts."

"George Washington Carver made a compost heap even before I did!" said Harry.

"And his worked!" said Ivan loudly.

"I think Booker T. Washington would have for-given me," said Harry, "for writing the wrong re-port. Because he believed in learning from your mistakes. Right, Mrs. Ott?"

Mrs. Ott laughed. "Learning is learning," she said. "Just look in your notebook next time."

After school, Harry and Dorothy walked home together. Chloe had gone to her friend's house, and the two of them walked slowly, breathing in the fresh air.

"Mrs. Pell's forsythia bush is starting to get flowers," said Harry. "Spring is really here."

"How do you remember the names of the flow-ers?" said Dorothy, impressed.

"I like to learn," said Harry cheerfully. "Like George and Booker T."

"Who's that sitting on the front porch?" said Dorothy.

"It's Mama!" said Harry, running toward her.

"Arney's sleeping," Mrs. Kane whispered as she gave Harry a hug. "I thought you'd like a picnic snack outside." She pulled a can out of a paper bag and pried off the lid.

"Take some," she said to Harry. "And a juice box, too."

Harry smiled widely as he popped a handful of peanuts into his mouth. "Delicious," he said.

"Yummy," said Dorothy, sipping on a juice box.

"Did you know," said Harry, crunching loudly, "that I slept on the floor last night to see what it felt like to be born a slave?"

Mrs. Kane rolled her eyes. "You scared the daylights out of me," she said. "I went in to check on the baby, and you were missing from your bed!"

Dorothy chimed in. "I heard Mom yell, 'Henry, Henry, Harry is missing!'"

"And what happened?" said Harry.

"Your father brought me my glasses, and we found you."

"Were you happy to see me?" Harry stopped chewing for a second.

"Of course we were," said Mrs. Kane, leaning over to hug Harry again.

"It seems like Arney is the one you care about the most," said Harry.

"Arney is a baby, sweetheart. He can't do anything for himself. Not like you can."

"It's true," said Harry. "I can do a lot. I can make my own compost heap. I can make new friends, like Dr. Arney and Jared at the hospital. I can get rid of a bat for Grandma." Harry put his hand in the can again and smiled widely. "Did you know that George Washington Carver made shampoo out of these?" he said, pointing to the metal can.

"No kidding," said Mrs. Kane, smiling as broadly as Harry. "Tell me all about it."

And Harry did, in between munching on handfuls of peanuts as they sat in the sunshine while Arney slept.

6

Like Son, Like Father

"WHAT ARE WE DOING today?" Harry asked as Mr. Kane slid two pieces of French toast onto his plate.

"Ask your mother," said Harry's father grouchily.

"We're going on a trip to visit my old college friend Karin," said Mrs. Kane, putting Arney in his swing seat and arranging a blanket around his head.

"She has a new baby," said Mr. Kane, rolling his eyes. "As if we don't have enough noise with Arney around. Now we have to go and visit some more noise."

"I told you I'd go by myself," said Mrs. Kane, winding up the swing. She watched as Arney started rocking back and forth, click click, click click. "He loves the rhythm," she said, pouring herself a cup of coffee.

"Watch me," said Harry, chewing loudly in time to the clicking noise. "I like rhythm, too!"

"Please don't," said Mrs. Kane. "You could choke."

"Please don't gross me out," added Chloe.

Harry jabbed at another piece of French toast. "What about Arney?" he said. "He could throw up in front of our eyes, couldn't he? And I haven't eaten my breakfast yet!"

"He won't do a thing but rock," promised Harry's mother as his sisters groaned loudly.

Mrs. Kane took a container out of the refrigerator and poured some yellow liquid and a splash of milk into a bowl.

"What's that goop?" said Harry.

"Fake eggs," said Mrs. Kane. "For people like me with high cholesterol." She ignored the groans and dipped a piece of whole-wheat bread into the mixture. "Is it my imagination," she said, spraying some fake butter onto a pan, "or did the whole family wake up on the wrong side of the bed?"

"Arney's happy!" said Harry, rocking his head in time to the swing.

The skillet sizzled as Mrs. Kane placed the piece of bread on it and sprinkled some cinnamon on top.

Harry sniffed. "Smells good," he said. "Did I tell you that my cholesterol is five trillion million?"

"You've had two pieces already," said Mrs. Kane. "Go get dressed so we can leave soon."

"Do we have to go?" Chloe whined. "Mei-Hua invited me to spend the day at her house."

"Don't start copying me," said Mr. Kane. "We'll all go without fussing."

"Why would I want to visit another screaming baby?" said Chloe, making a face.

"You look like a bulldog," said Harry.

"I do not!" shouted Chloe.

"She does not!" cried Dorothy.

"Children!" Mr. Kane raised his hands. "Let's all start over. Chloe?"

Chloe sighed. Then she rearranged the mad look on her face and said sweetly, "Oh, I'd love to go, but would you mind very much if I stayed home and played with my best friend Mei-Hua? Pretty please with a cherry on top?"

"That's better," said Mr. Kane, laughing. "Did her mother invite you?"

"It gives us more room in the car," said Mrs. Kane, flipping her piece of fake-egg French toast onto a plate.

"I could give you more room, too," said Harry, eyeing his mother's French toast. "I could stay home and play with Benjamin."

His mother smiled and said, "We'd like the pleasure of your company, Harry, and no, you cannot eat my French toast."

Dorothy piped up. "Grandma said she'd take me to the movies!" She stood up and pushed back her chair as dramatically as she could without knocking it over. "It's no fair! Harry had a special day with her, the day he found the bat, and I've been waiting forever and ever for my special day."

"Let's start over," said Harry, imitating his parents, who had read in a book that if your children were fresh, you should ask them to try again until they got it right.

Chloe smirked, but Dorothy said huffily, "Only Mom and Dad are allowed to tell me to start over."

"Start over," said Mrs. Kane, picking up the telephone and dialing a number. "Dad? Is it true that Mom offered to take Dorothy to the movies today?" She cupped her hand over the receiver and said, "He's asking Grandma."

"Were you lying?" Harry said to Dorothy.

"Maybe it wasn't today, but she said she'd take me," said Dorothy quickly.

"She was lying," said Harry. "She just doesn't want to go on the trip."

"I hate you, Harry Kane," said Dorothy. "You're despicable."

"Mama says not to use the word hate," said Harry, thinking that Arney's crying was a lot better than Dorothy's whining. "And I'm not despicable or despannable or whatever you called me."

Chloe hooted with laughter. "He's getting Spic

and Span mixed up with despicable!" she said, digging an elbow into Dorothy's ribs.

"What a dodo!" cried Dorothy.

Harry felt his face turn red. Only yesterday, the entire class had laughed uproariously when Mrs. Ott had asked them, "Who knows about odds and evens?" Harry knew the answer and had called out, "They were the first people on earth that God created!"—only it wasn't meant to be a joke. The class laughed until lunchtime.

Harry was just about to crash out of the room and maybe bang into Dorothy on the way, when he heard his mother say, "Laura is there? How come she didn't tell me?"

"Aunt Laura is at Grandma's?" said Harry. "I'm going to Grandma's, too."

Dorothy glared at him. "It's my special day, not yours."

"But Aunt Laura is at Grandma's," said Harry.

"It's all settled," said Mrs. Kane, hanging up the telephone. "Chloe, you're staying with Mei-Hua. Dorothy, you're going to the movies with

Grandma. And Harry, you are going with Arney and Dad and me and Laura to visit my old school friend in New Jersey, who has a new baby."

"Your sister is coming with us to Karin's house?" said Mr. Kane, raising an eyebrow. "She'd better not smoke in the car."

"Karin has her brother visiting, and he's not married," said Mrs. Kane.

"And you want him to marry Aunt Laura?" said Harry.

"We'll see," said Mrs. Kane, smiling as she wound up Arney's swing again.

Mr. Kane said he didn't need a map to find the town of Mountain Lakes because he knew roughly where it was. They had two hours to reach it, plenty of time to arrive for a one o'clock lunch. By the time they had dropped Chloe off at Mei-Hua's house, and Dorothy at Grandma's house with hugs and kisses for Aunt Laura, Arney had stopped crying in his car seat and was sleeping peacefully.

Harry felt lucky because Aunt Laura sat next to

him in the backseat. With Arney asleep, he had her all to himself.

"Mama wants you to marry her friend's brother," Harry announced.

"She does, does she?" said Laura, smiling.

"You don't have the little crinkles around your eyes that my mother has," said Harry.

Mr. Kane snorted in the front seat, and Harry's mother gave him a playful jab.

"No hitting, children," said Laura, and his mother straightened up in her seat. "I'm younger than your mother," Laura said to Harry. "I'll be getting wrinkles soon enough."

"Laugh lines and worry lines," said Mrs. Kane. "You'll get them when you have children."

Laura and Mrs. Kane talked for a long time about Arney's constant crying and Laura's new job in the city and what Karin's brother looked like and where he lived in case he and Laura liked each other.

Harry concentrated on counting gas stations. "Seven, eight, nine . . . Hey, Dad," said Harry. "We're going around in circles."

"Are we lost?" said Mrs. Kane, rummaging in the glove compartment for a map. "I knew I should have brought the road map."

"We're not lost, we're sightseeing," said Mr. Kane.

"Pull over and we'll ask someone at the gas station."

"I'll find it."

"This happens every time we go on a long trip."

"I know where it is. I just have to get my bearings."

Mrs. Kane turned around and said to Laura, "Why is it that men won't ask for directions?"

"I read an article about that in the newspaper," said Laura. "They think they're supposed to know. It's pride or something."

"Do you think you know where we are?" Harry tapped his father on the shoulder.

"I'll find it," his father repeated.

They drove some more. Harry was about to open his mouth and tell his father that he would ask for directions when Mrs. Kane sat bolt upright in her seat and said, "Pull into that gas station this minute,

Henry, or I won't speak to you for the rest of the day!"

Mr. Kane did as he was told, and Harry watched his mother jump out of the car and speak to a man through a hole in a glass booth.

Mrs. Kane got back into the car. "It's not far," she said. "Make a left-hand turn."

It was one o'clock when Mr. Kane passed a sign that said MOUNTAIN LAKE, and it was one-thirty by the time Mrs. Kane told him once more, quite firmly, that he had better turn into the next gas station to ask for directions to Hillside Crescent, where Karin lived.

A man by the gas pump took off his cap and scratched his head. "I've lived here for twenty-seven years," he said. "I don't ever recall that name."

Arney started to cry noisily, and Mrs. Kane jumped out of the car, rummaging in her pocket for a piece of paper. "It says here, 51 Hillside Crescent, Mountain Lakes."

"I just can't help you," said the man, waving them on so that he could give the car behind them some gas.

"I'll call Karin," said Mrs. Kane, slamming the door so hard that Arney started to scream.

"I see what she means about Arney's crying," said Aunt Laura.

"Hold on to your eardrums," said Harry.

Mrs. Kane returned and said grimly, "It's Mountain Lakes we want."

"So where's Hillside Crescent?" said Laura, jiggling Arney's car seat so that his cries became whimpers.

"In Mountain Lakes!" said Mrs. Kane. "We are two hours away, in a totally different town called Mountain Lake."

Harry thought he heard his father gulp. Mr. Kane started up the car engine without a word.

"Make a right turn and get back on the highway," said Mrs. Kane coldly. "I've got directions, something I should have gotten in the first place."

"Why don't we just go home?" Mr. Kane said grouchily.

"Children!" said Laura cheerfully.

"Let's start over," said Harry.

Arney cried louder.

"I need to meet the man I'm going to marry!" joked Aunt Laura, but Harry's mother and father didn't smile.

"It's okay, Dad," said Harry. "We all make mistakes."

"Thank you, son," said his father.

"Mrs. Ott asked us about odds and evens, and I thought she was talking about Adam and Eve in the Garden of Eden." Harry waited. No one laughed. No one even giggled.

Mrs. Kane shifted in her seat. "Odds and evens?" she said.

"Like two, four, six, eight?" said Mr. Kane.

"Adam and Eve," said Harry. This time he was delighted when Mrs. Kane started to laugh, and Mr. Kane joined her. They couldn't possibly laugh until lunchtime, because lunchtime turned into suppertime by the time they reached Mountain Lakes.

"We ate already!" said Karin. "We just couldn't wait any longer!"

"Don't worry," said Mrs. Kane, unbuckling Arney and pulling him out of the car seat. "I'm so sorry we're late."

"I'm starving!" said Harry.

Mr. Kane stayed in the car. "I'll tell you what," he said. "We passed a supermarket on the way here. I'll go get us some cold cuts and rolls, and you won't have to go to any trouble."

"I'll go, too," said Harry, climbing into the front seat.

Mrs. Kane poked her head inside the window. "Get some paper plates, honey," she said.

"She's not mad at you anymore, is she, Dad?"

"I don't think so, Harry," said his father as he backed out of the driveway.

Harry followed Mr. Kane's red-and-black-checked woolen jacket into the supermarket. Mrs. Kane said Harry's father looked like a deer hunter in it, but it was his father's favorite article of clothing, perfect for gardening and hiking.

Pathmark supermarket was at least a block long. Harry thought maybe people ate more in New Jersey. He followed his father past the biggest display of cereal boxes he had ever seen. He counted four kinds of cereal with marshmallow bits in them, but he had to stop counting how many cereals had oats in them because his father's black-and-red jacket had disappeared around the corner.

Harry stood behind his father on the deli line. He counted eighteen types of cheese, five different kinds of bologna, eleven bins of salads, and fourteen different kinds of rolls. Then Mr. Kane was leaving, and Harry quickly followed him down the aisle, gazing wide-eyed at a wall of candy as he paced himself behind the black-and-red flash that was his father.

Except that it wasn't his father. As they reached the exit, Harry spied a gumball machine. "Dad!" he called loudly, and the man in the black-and-red jacket didn't turn around, but Harry saw his profile as he stepped onto the runway that flipped the doors open automatically. The man had a mustache. Harry's father didn't.

Harry froze. He turned around and retraced his steps past the gumball machine, which no longer interested him, past the array of candy and the wall of cereal, to the back of the store with the big red letters that spelled DELI.

His father was nowhere to be seen. Harry sped down another aisle, past stacks of diapers and baby food and Vaseline and pacifiers and yellow rubber ducks and clear plastic baby bottles. He thought of Arney. Arney needed his big brother Harry, so he had to find his father because he couldn't be lost forever in a supermarket in New Jersey.

Harry caught a flash of red as he ran down the next aisle, but it was a woman in a red suit who looked nothing like his father, and now he was caught in a sea of laundry detergent, including the kind with the lavender scent that his mother bought, and if he didn't find his father soon, he'd never smell that lavender scent again. And maybe they wouldn't even miss a grouchy boy who chewed in time to the clicking noise with his mouth wide open, who grossed out his sisters and complained about his brother, and who wanted to eat up his mother's cholesterol-free French toast. Maybe they wouldn't miss him at all.

Harry stopped in his tracks. He took a deep

breath and ordered his brain to start thinking scientifically. If he kept running up and down the aisles, he might never find his father. He walked toward the front of the store and spotted a tall booth with a sign above it.

"Cus . . ." Harry tried to sound out the name, but it was too hard. Cuss words in a supermarket? No way. Custard? There was no ice cream or pudding to be seen. Harry tapped on the wall of the booth and said, "Excuse me."

A man was moving around up there, but he didn't hear Harry. Harry took a deep breath and said loudly, "Excuse me, but I'm lost!"

"Lost?" said the man, peering over the counter to look at Harry. "What's your name, and who are you looking for?"

"Harry Kane," said Harry. "They used to call me Hurricane Harry, but maybe you should just say that Harry is looking for his father, Henry Kane. My mother calls him Henry when she's mad at him."

The man smiled and spoke into a microphone. "We have a lost boy at the customer service desk called Harry, who is looking for his father, Henry Kane."

"My brother's name is Arney," added Harry. "He needs me."

The man spoke into the microphone again. "He says his brother Arney needs him." The message reverberated through the supermarket, and in less than a minute, a black-and-red jacket came bounding into view, but his father's smiling face was all that Harry really saw.

"What happened?" said Mr. Kane, scooping Harry up and giving him a hug.

"I followed the wrong red-and-black jacket out of the store," said Harry.

Mr. Kane took Harry's hand, and they walked back to the deli section to pick up their groceries. "I just realized something," said Mr. Kane, crouching down in the cake-mix aisle and cupping Harry's round face in his hands. "You don't take after me," he said.

Harry looked injured. "I do, too," he said. "We both like basketball, and we both like tapioca pudding and cowboy movies and—"

Mr. Kane laughed. "I mean, you take after me when it comes to some of the good things, but not the bad. I got us totally lost by not asking anyone for directions. And what did you do?"

"I got lost, too," said Harry. "But I asked for help."

"That's right!" said Mr. Kane, standing up. "You must be very proud of yourself."

"It just takes practice," said Harry. "I need help . . ." Harry pulled a brownie mix off the shelf next to him. "Making brownies!" Harry examined the box. "You can help me read the directions," he added.

"I'll not only read them," said Mr. Kane, "I'll follow them!" He put the mix in his basket and walked with Harry to the checkout counter. "Watch this," he whispered to Harry as the clerk rang up their items. His voice got louder. "Could you tell me how to get back to the highway from here?" Mr. Kane listened carefully and tweaked Harry's hand.

"You're getting good, Dad," said Harry.

"Like son, like father," said Mr. Kane.

7

The B.O.N.G. Club

WHEN HARRY and his father told Mrs. Kane about Harry's adventure in the supermarket, her eyes popped out of her head like marbles.

"At least he asked for help," said Harry's father meekly. "He didn't walk around in circles like somebody I know."

"You didn't walk around in circles," said Harry helpfully. "You drove." Harry waved his new brownie mix in the air. "Dad says he'll practice following directions by making brownies with me." He turned to Karin and said, "Would you like me to make a special treat for your new baby?"

Karin looked doubtful. "I don't think Emily's up to eating brownies yet, Harry," she said.

"My father would eat them," said Harry. "They're his favorite dessert."

"The answer is no, Harry," said Mrs. Kane sharply. "I don't want you messing up Karin's kitchen."

"Karin has enough work on her hands with the new baby," said Aunt Laura in the same sharp tone.

Harry glared at his aunt. He hardly ever saw her, and she sounded just like his mother! He ignored his mother, whose first son was almost lost in the supermarket forever, and who didn't care enough to let him bake brownies! Harry stomped past the baby swing, skirted the changing table, and crouched in the corner of the living room. "It's not fair," he said in a muffled voice that the grown-ups could barely hear. "Arney messes up my room every day, and I never even asked for a new baby!"

"I'll help him," volunteered a man who was sitting quietly on the couch by Harry's corner. "I happen to love brownies myself."

Harry peeked at the man. His face was beet red except for the white circles around his eyes, but it was a nice craggy face like Harry's father's.

Harry clasped his hands together and pleaded, "Can I, Mom?"

"I'll supervise," said Aunt Laura eagerly. "We'll leave the kitchen spotless."

Mrs. Kane protested, but she couldn't stop Karin from leading the red-faced man, Aunt Laura, and Harry into the kitchen.

Karin rummaged in the cupboard and handed the red-faced man a metal pan. "I forgot how much you love brownies," she said.

A sudden wail erupted from the living room. Karin grabbed a measuring cup from the dish drainer and banged it on the table. "Preheat the oven," she said, rushing out of the kitchen.

"Where's the fire?" said the red-faced man.

"She thinks it's Emily crying," explained Harry, "but it's really Arney."

"He cries all the time," said Aunt Laura, opening up the brownie mix and handing the packet to Harry.

"Not all the time," said Harry defensively as he dumped the brown powder into the bowl that the red-faced man put in front of him. "He doesn't cry when he drinks his bottle."

"That handsome boy in the other room is your brother?" said the man, winking at Harry as he tied an apron around his waist. "He has a great set of lungs."

"Like mine," said Harry. "They'll come in handy someday, won't they?"

"Of course they will," said the man. "Just think how long he'll be able to swim underwater."

"And just think how loud he can yell at a baseball game," said Harry.

"With lungs like that, he could be a singer when he grows up."

"He won't need a microphone!" said Harry, laughing along with the red-faced man until it dawned on Harry who he was. "You're the one that my aunt Laura is supposed to meet!" he said.

"Harry!" said Aunt Laura, her cheeks flushed.

"She doesn't have the laugh lines and the worry lines that my mother has," continued Harry, "but she'll get them when she has children. Most of the time, she's really nice."

"I'm Karin's brother, George," said the man. "And I thought your aunt was nice the minute I saw her."

Harry examined George scientifically. "Why is your face so red?" he said.

George patted his cheeks gingerly. "It even hurts when I smile!" he said. "Never fall asleep under a sunlamp, Harry."

"Why did you go under a sunlamp?"

"To impress your aunt Laura with a tan," said George ruefully.

"My mother makes us wear sunscreen," said Harry. "Sunburn isn't good for your skin."

Laura sighed and took a packet of cigarettes out of her pocket.

Harry looked accusingly at his aunt as she removed a cigarette. "And smoking isn't, either," he said.

"Goodness, you sound just like your father," said Aunt Laura, putting the cigarette back in the packet. "I'm trying to quit."

Harry turned to George. "The secondhand smoke isn't good for us, either, my dad told me."

George burst out laughing. "Where did your sister hatch this one?" he said, hooking a thumb at Harry.

"I'm a mammal," said Harry solemnly. "I wasn't hatched."

George laughed until he had tears in his eyes. "You crack me up," he said, gasping as he pressed his hands against his red cheeks.

Harry held a finger in the air. "Which reminds me," he said. "Where's my egg?"

George produced a large white egg from a carton in the refrigerator and tapped it against the bowl. "Watch the master chef at work," he said.

"I feel like I'm watching Laurel and Hardy," said Aunt Laura as Harry made a drumroll with two wooden spoons and George held the egg aloft. The liquid plopped into the middle of the bowl.

"Now we're all cracked," said Harry happily as he rotated the wooden spoon and mixed in the egg with gusto.

*　*　*

Everybody ate Mr. Kane's bologna sandwiches and complimented Harry on his chewy brownies. Arney sat in a little seat next to Emily. Arney squawked while he waved his hands and kicked his feet. Emily sat very still and peeped.

"Those are happy noises," Harry told George. He could see that George didn't know very much about babies because George refused to hold either Arney or Emily.

Arney screeched a little louder.

George complimented Arney on his lungs again.

"He's not an easy baby," said Mrs. Kane. "Dorothy and Chloe and Harry were more like Emily. As good as gold."

"He's talking," snapped Harry as he wrapped three pieces of bologna in a napkin. "He's trying to tell us something."

Arney screwed up his face and formed a wide O with his mouth.

Harry tucked the bologna package into his pocket and regarded his brother scientifically. "Hmm," said Harry.

"What now?" said George, leaning toward Harry. "A Bronx cheer?"

Harry shook his head. "He's either making poo-poo or he's going to cry."

Arney let out a wail that frightened Emily so much that she started to whimper.

"Even her crying is quieter," said Karin, joining in.

Harry sniffed. "As a scientist," he said, "I know exactly why he's crying."

"Why?" said Mrs. Kane, lifting Arney out of his seat.

Harry looked at his mother, who began bouncing Arney up and down, then at his aunt, who was shaking a rattle in his baby brother's face, and finally at Karin, who was holding Emily away from Arney's screaming. It was clear to Harry that they did not appreciate Arney's powerful lungs. It was clear to Harry that they did not appreciate Arney at all.

"He doesn't like girls," Harry announced.

"Is that so?" said George, nodding his head solemnly. "Then maybe we boys had better stick together."

"I think so," said Harry.

On the drive back home, Arney sat in his car seat, eyes wide open and fists clenched. He didn't make a peep.

"I was right, wasn't I?" Harry whispered to his brother.

Arney continued staring at the ceiling.

"Wasn't George nice?" Aunt Laura said to no one in particular.

"Very nice," said Mrs. Kane, turning in her seat to look anxiously at Arney. "Why is he so quiet?"

"He feels better," said Harry. "He knows I understand."

"I can't get over how good Karin's baby was," said Aunt Laura, who knew that she had said the wrong thing when Harry snorted loudly in the seat next to her.

At last Arney fell asleep. Laura started chattering about George again. "We're going for a walk in Central Park next week."

"I could go with you," said Harry. "I like parks."

"I don't think so," said Aunt Laura. "We want to get to know each other."

"I could help you," said Harry.

"Harry!" said Mrs. Kane.

"He'd have a better time with me," muttered Harry.

"What was that?" said Mr. Kane sternly, looking at Harry with eagle eyes through the rearview mirror.

Harry pressed his lips together and didn't say another word until they reached his grandmother's apartment building.

Dorothy appeared and waited for Aunt Laura to get out of the car. She scrunched in next to Harry. "It smells funny in here," she said, sniffing Harry's shirt sleeve. "You smell like bologna."

"Why don't you go back to Grandma's house?" said Harry, wondering if his package of bologna was too squashed to eat.

"Good-bye!" said Laura, the very aunt who wouldn't take him to Central Park with her.

"Have a nice time with George," said Mrs. Kane, the mother who let him write a report about

George Washington Carver instead of Booker T. Washington.

"You really smell," said Dorothy, the most annoying sister in the world until Chloe got into the car.

"I didn't have that much fun," complained Chloe. "We got fruit for dessert."

"Fruit is good for you," said Mrs. Kane.

"We had brownies," said Harry helpfully.

"And you didn't save any for me?" said Chloe, scowling.

"Or me?" said Dorothy. "Grandma thought I was Harry and made yicky tapioca pudding!"

"Yuck!" said Chloe.

"It was disgusting!" said Dorothy.

Arney started screaming.

"Now see what you did!" said Harry, patting his brother's head as he dug an elbow into Dorothy's ribs.

"He's crying because he's sitting next to a stinky bologna brother!" said Dorothy, elbowing Harry back.

Chloe laughed out loud in the front seat. Harry

regarded one sister with the hyena laugh and the other sister with the elbow in his ribs and his mother anxiously watching Arney. George was absolutely right. Boys had better stick together.

Harry made up his mind. He was going to start his very own club, and he knew exactly who wouldn't be allowed to join it. Girls.

Dorothy and Chloe were no sweeter to Harry in the morning. Dorothy accused her brother of taking the waffle with the most syrup on it. She continued calling him bologna brother.

"You'll be sorry," said Harry.

Chloe couldn't find her library book. "It was on reptiles, Harry. Did you steal it?"

"Stick a hose up your nose," said Harry, trying out the new expression that Ivan Seeger had used on him.

"Mommmm! Harry's saying nasty things to me."

"I am not," said Harry. "A hose would never fit up a nose anyway."

"Watch it, Harry," said Mrs. Kane, cradling Arney.

"Watch what?" said Harry. "The birds in the sky?"

"Any more fresh talk, and you'll be watching the walls in your room," said his mother.

"You mean you want me to stay home from school?" said Harry, his voice trailing off as his mother gave him a warning look.

By the time Harry arrived at Walnut School, he was relieved to see Benjamin, a friend and a boy, in the school yard.

"How would you like to start a club with me?" he said.

"Neat," said Benjamin.

"A boys' club," added Harry. "No girls are allowed."

"Neat," repeated Benjamin. "We can make a list of them."

"A list of what?" The familiar voice of Ivan Seeger breathed in Harry's right ear.

"A list of the girls that aren't allowed in our club," said Harry.

"Great," said Ivan. "Sally Freed goes on the list. She says she can run faster than me."

"She can," said Harry.

"He's right," echoed Benjamin.

"She thinks she's better in math than I am!"

"She is!" said Harry.

"Well," Ivan growled. "She sings to me in the morning, and now I don't have to listen."

After school, the boys arranged to play at Benjamin's house. They asked Mrs. Tuttle for three pieces of paper.

"You're doing your homework, boys?" said Mrs. Tuttle. "That's terrific."

Benjamin looked doubtful as she walked away. "It will be hard not to talk to my mother," he whispered.

"Not for me," said Ivan. "If my mother tells me one more time to clean up my room, I'll . . ."

"Mother's aren't on the list," Harry said firmly. He had given it a great deal of thought. "Or grandmothers or aunts or teachers. Besides, they're not really girls."

"What about sisters?" said Benjamin. "And what's our signal if a girl comes around?"

"Sisters are definitely on the list," said Harry, wondering if Chloe's reptile book was in his desk at school.

"Oink," said Ivan. "Oink is a good signal if a girl comes around."

Harry shook his head. "My mother wouldn't like it," he said. "How about beep?"

"That's good," said Benjamin.

"Let's call ourselves the I Hate Girls Club," said Ivan.

"My mother doesn't let us use the word hate around the house," said Benjamin. "How about Boys Only?"

Harry wrote the words on a piece of paper. "I've got it!" he said, writing down two more words. "How about Boys Only, No Girls? B.O.N.G. for short."

Benjamin and Ivan wrote B.O.N.G. at the top of their papers, and they changed the signal for girls coming around from beep to bong. Then they went outside to look for girls.

* * *

The B.O.N.G. Club did not work well at school. If Mrs. Ott noticed Harry ignoring a particular girl, she would arch an eyebrow and stare at Harry in a manner that reminded Harry very much of his mother.

At home for dinner, Harry made believe he had laryngitis when Dorothy asked him if Ivan Seeger had a crush on Sally Freed. "He's always running after her in the school yard," she said. "But it's obvious she doesn't like him one bit."

Harry pointed to his throat and didn't reply, but when the vanilla fudge ice cream appeared on the table, he shouted, "Two scoops for me!" His mother commented that it was odd how Harry's laryngitis cleared up at the sight of ice cream.

The next morning at school, Harry discovered that Dorothy was right. Ivan Seeger was chasing Sally Freed all over the school yard. There was nothing in the club rules that said he couldn't, but when Ivan Seeger's hand was an inch away from pulling Sally Freed's ponytail, he didn't yell

"Bong!" the way he was supposed to. He pulled her hair instead.

Sally yanked her ponytail away and turned to face him with her hands on her hips. Harry couldn't help admiring how Sally Freed was not in the least bit afraid of Ivan the Terrible Seeger. In a loud singsong voice she chanted:

> "My mother, your mother, live across the
>   street,
> Eighteen, nineteen, Mulberry Street,
> Every night they have a fight
> And this is what they say.
> Boys are rotten, made out of cotton,
> Girls are dandy, made out of candy,
> Boys go to Jupiter to get more stupider,
> Girls go to college to get more knowledge,
> Boys drink Slice to get more lice,
> Girls hardly drink 'cause they'd rather
>   think!"

By the end of the song, a crowd of girls and boys had gathered. Sally lifted her chin up, flipped back her ponytail, and stuck her tongue out at Ivan.

Then she took Jessica Weinstein's arm and they flounced off together.

As the president of the B.O.N.G. Club, Harry tried to look at the problem scientifically. Why would Ivan, whom Harry considered to be treasurer of the B.O.N.G. Club because he got more allowance than anyone else, chase after Sally every morning in the school yard? Harry made up his mind to tell the treasurer after school that it was not a girl-chasing club at all. It was more of a running-away-from-girls club, and pulling hair was against the rules.

It was after school that the trouble began. Walking down the hallway, Harry peered into the science room to say hello to Boarshead, the classroom hamster. A few hours before, Harry's class had examined the different parts of Boarshead's body. Today's focus had been the eye. Mr. Gezzik had cradled in his hand a beautiful glass replica of the human eye. He had held it so gently that Harry was reminded of Dorothy with her favorite baby doll. Then with a pointer that resembled a pick-up stick, he had shown them the iris and the cornea and the pupil and had carefully placed the glass eye back on its special mahogany stand.

Harry glanced at Mr. Gezzik's desk. There was his science teacher's favorite mug, his seating plan with the Yankees sticker on it, his African violet in the plastic Mets cap, the apple he hadn't had time to eat, and the special mahogany stand that held the beautiful glass eye . . . except that the beautiful glass eye was gone.

Ivan and Benjamin liked holding the B.O.N.G. Club at Harry's house because there were more girls at Harry's house to ignore. Whenever Dorothy or Chloe passed their brother's bedroom on the way to the bathroom, the boys yelled, "Bong!" Dorothy twirled a finger and pointed it at her head, saying, "Cuckoo!" Chloe just called them bird-brains.

"How can we be birdbrains?" said Harry from the doorway. "We're mammals."

"How about bat brains?" said Chloe, who was never at a loss for words. "You're big on bats, aren't you, Harry?"

"We're not supposed to talk to them," whispered Benjamin.

Harry and the boys retreated to the bedroom and began work on their official B.O.N.G. Club notebook. Harry took his pencil and wrote "Why boys are better" at the top of the page. Then he drew a line down the middle of the page and printed the word "Boys" on one side and "Girls" on the other.

"Dirt!" said Benjamin. "We like dirt better than girls do."

Under the boys heading, Harry wrote "durt."

"Write 'Girls are cleaner' on the other side," said Ivan.

Harry was doubtful. "Dorothy is pretty clean," he said. "But Chloe is sloppy, like me."

"Smart!" said Ivan. "Boys are smarter."

Harry cocked his head to the side. "Do you think so?" he said. "Chloe is as smart as an eagle."

"But who's smarter?" said Benjamin.

"I'll write it down," said Harry, "but I'm not so sure. Chloe gets straight As." Harry's tongue stuck out of the corner of his mouth as he concentrated.

He was sure he had spelled the word "dirt" wrong, and "smarter" was even harder. Dorothy was good at spelling, and it was all that he could do to stop himself from calling out to her in the next room.

"Write down 'fun,' " said Benjamin. "Boys have more fun."

Harry was relieved. "Fun" he could spell, but just as he was writing it down, the pencil point broke right off and flew across the table.

"I'll get another pencil," said Ivan, rooting at the bottom of his knapsack for one. "I've got one in here somewhere." He held the knapsack upside down until six pennies, a key chain, a troll doll, two pencils, and a beautiful glass eye fell out of the bag directly onto the carpet.

Ivan moved quickly, cupping the glass eye in his hand and shoving it back into the knapsack. "That's Sally Freed's troll doll," he said hastily, pointing to the doll. "She sang that stupid song again today, and I took it out of her desk."

"Sports," said Benjamin, who obviously didn't see a thing. "Write down 'sports.' "

Harry felt as though his heart was rolling around in his stomach, right next to the two pretzel rods, three Oreo cookies, and five slices of apple that he'd had for snack. Who cared if Ivan Seeger chased after Sally Freed? He could chase after the wind and the stars, for all Harry cared. Harry felt sick. How could Ivan take Mr. Gezzik's beautiful glass eye? Harry steadied the hand that gripped the pencil with the broken point. He wanted with all his heart to write down "Mr. Gezzik's glass eye" in bright red Magic Marker. And after that, "Ivan the Terrible took it."

Harry handed Benjamin the notebook. "Write down whatever you want," he said faintly.

It was a relief when the doorbell rang, and Mrs. Tuttle arrived to pick up Benjamin and Ivan. "Your mother says to tell you that she's fixed your favorite dinner today, Ivan," said Mrs. Tuttle.

Ivan patted his stomach. "G and G," he said, closing his knapsack.

"What's that?" said Benjamin as he followed his mother out the door.

Ivan laughed and called after him, "Grease and garbage!" Then he dragged Harry into a corner and snarled, "You'd better not tell anyone about the eye." Ivan's voice turned into a fierce whisper. "If you breathe a word, I'll tell Mr. Gezzik that it was your idea for the B.O.N.G. Club and that we had to steal something to belong. I'll tell him that you took Sally Freed's troll doll and that you made me take something, too. So if you want to stay out of trouble, keep your mouth shut." He followed Benjamin out of the bedroom and uttered a single "Bong!" as he bumped into Chloe.

"Hey, Harry!" Ivan called from the doorway. "Catch!" he said, throwing Sally Freed's troll doll so hard that it sailed past Harry and landed on the bed. "You can have it!" yelled Ivan. Then he turned around and was gone.

Chloe peered into Harry's room and said, "He really is a bat brain, you know."

"I know," said Harry miserably.

"What's the matter, Harry?" Chloe came in and shut the door.

Harry shook his head. "I'm not supposed to talk to you," he said sadly.

"Oh." Chloe patted Harry's knee. "Make believe I'm a boy," she said.

"How did you find out about the club?" said Harry.

"I'm a sneak," said Chloe. "I read it on a piece of paper."

Harry looked into his big sister's brown eyes. They didn't look sneaky at all. They looked kind. "It's—it's against the rules," said Harry, his own eyes filling with tears.

"Rules can be broken if it's important enough," said Chloe.

"Or if they're stupid rules," said Harry hopefully.

"So tell me, Harry."

Chloe's eyes looked smart now, as smart as an eagle's, and Harry took a deep breath and the words came tumbling out in a rush. "What would you do if someone you knew stole something from somebody and you could get in big trouble if you said anything?"

Chloe cupped her chin in her hand. She narrowed her eyes. She wrinkled up her aquiline nose. Finally she said, "I think I would have to tell."

"But that's squealing," said Harry. "I don't think Mr. Gezzik likes squealers."

"I don't think he likes stealing and lying, either," said Chloe. "Think about it."

Harry couldn't sleep that night. There were no bats in the corner of his room to keep him awake. There were no monsters under his bed to keep him wide-eyed and trembling like the baby he used to be. He wasn't a baby anymore. He was a big boy now. What would he tell his little brother Arney to do? He listened carefully to the baby's gentle breathing in the crib on the other side of the room. It was as rhythmic as music, and it calmed him.

Harry made up his mind. He didn't believe in stealing and he didn't want to lie. If he wanted his brother to be proud of him, he knew what he had to do. He would tell Mr. Gezzik in the morning.

Dorothy and Chloe were especially kind to Harry at breakfast. Dorothy switched waffles and gave her brother the one with the most syrup. Chloe asked

Harry in a whisper if he wanted her to talk to Mr. Gezzik for him.

"No, thanks," Harry whispered back. "I can do it myself." He chewed on a particularly syrupy piece of waffle. "Did you tell Dorothy?" he added.

"She knows," said Chloe out loud.

"And I can guess which pea brain we're talking about," said Dorothy.

Harry waited until Mr. Gezzik finished giving his science lesson. He waited until his science teacher sat down at the desk that held the special mahogany stand that was empty. Mr. Gezzik stood up. He cleared his throat and began to speak.

"Someone has taken my glass eye," he began. Joey Ward tittered, and Mr. Gezzik rapped his knuckles so hard on his desk that the pencils clattered in the I LOVE MY SCIENCE TEACHER mug. The room was totally silent except for the scuttling of Boarshead in his cage.

Mr. Gezzik continued. "Perhaps he or she borrowed it. Perhaps he or she thought it would make a good paperweight. But it's mine and I miss it and I'd like it back. Whoever knows the whereabouts of my glass eye, please report to me after school. There will be no questions asked."

Benjamin ate his usual peanut butter on rye bread for lunch. Ivan managed to down a tuna-fish sandwich and a chocolate-covered doughnut with a carton of milk. Harry could barely swallow. He stuffed his half-eaten lunch back into his lunch box and stood up.

"Don't do it," said Ivan through a milk-mustached mouth.

"Don't do what?" said Benjamin.

"Don't wait for me after school," said Harry as he followed the rest of his class out of the cafeteria.

At three o'clock, Harry stood outside Mr. Gezzik's classroom. He clutched Sally Freed's troll doll in one hand and knocked with the other. Harry loved science and discovery and compost heaps and mammals and bugs and bats, but today he wished he was anywhere else in the world than outside Mr. Gezzik's science room.

The door swung open, and Sally Freed appeared in the doorway.

"I told him," she said simply. "I saw Ivan take it, and I told Mr. Gezzik."

"Oh," said Harry, speechless, with his hands dangling at his sides.

"I'll take that," said Sally, reaching for the troll doll. "He stole that from me, too."

"I know," said Harry. "I brought it in to give it back to you."

Sally cocked her head to one side, so that her ponytail dangled in the air. "I like you, Harry. I like bats and bugs, too. So how come you want to hang around with a boy like Ivan?" Then she tucked her troll doll under her arm, and without waiting for an answer, walked away humming.

Harry watched her walk down the hallway, her ponytail swinging. Harry remembered what Grandpa Leon had told him about Grandma Rebecca: "I knew she was the one, the moment I saw her. She was the cat's meow."

Harry watched Sally as she turned the corner. "She's the cat's meow," he whispered.

* * *

Harry Kane walked home with his sisters.

"I went to tell Mr. Gezzik," said Harry, "and Sally Freed was there already. She's not afraid of anything."

"See?" said Chloe. "Girls aren't so bad."

When they got inside, Chloe fixed Harry a snack. Then she put on his favorite cartoon show, the one that she had boycotted the year before.

Mrs. Kane watched in amazement as Dorothy took the baby's smelly diaper pail out of Harry's room and emptied it. "I know how you hate the smell in your room," she said, pinching her nose together with her fingers so that her voice came out funny. Harry and Chloe held their noses, too, and they all started laughing at the noises they made.

"You children are the loves of my life," said Mrs. Kane out loud.

"Harry had a very hard day," explained Dorothy, sitting down next to her brother.

Harry sat on the couch, with Dorothy on one side of him and Chloe on the other. Chloe's head turned sharply as Arney started bawling in the next room. Her long hair whipped Harry in the face, but he didn't say a word. Dorothy sneezed, an inch from Harry's ear. He didn't wipe his cheek and yell, "Gross!" He didn't even dig an elbow into her ribs.

"I'll go," Harry said to his mother, clambering off the couch and running into his bedroom.

"Don't lift him," Mrs. Kane called after him.

Arney's crying stopped abruptly as Harry stuck his face over the crib railing. "Wait one second," he said to the baby. Harry took the B.O.N.G. Club notebook off his desk and leaned over Arney in the crib. Then he flicked the pages of the notebook so that a soft breeze tickled his brother's face. Arney puckered up his lips, scissored his feet, and smiled.

Harry threw the notebook into the wastebasket. He pressed his face against the crib railing, fitting his mouth between the bars. "I know why you cry so much," he whispered. "I've figured it out. It's not because you don't like girls. Girls can be nice. Sally Freed is the greatest, and Dorothy and Chloe love you almost as much as I do."

Harry stuck his hand between the railings and stroked his brother's soft round cheeks, cheeks that were as round as Harry's. "You're crying because it's hard being a boy," whispered Harry. "And it is. Just remember that I'm here to help you, because I've learned a lot this year."

Arney shut his eyes. Harry pulled the blue cover with the ducks on it up to his baby brother's chin and closed the bedroom door gently.

"He's lucky to have you," said Harry's mother from the hallway.

"I know," said Harry, and he sat down in between his sisters on the couch to watch the rest of his program.